DARCY'S DAYS

and Private thoughts

Vol. IV

Beginning November 1796

1 Nov (Tuesday)   Netherfield, Hertfordshire

The fresh page of a new volume finds me feet propped on a stool
broadside to the fire. Bingley ordered such a roaring blaze for
my room my ink dries ere it leaves the quill. I am arrived at his
leased estate an afternoon's ride north from the stable in
Marylebone. Heeler nuzzles oats below; I nuzzle brandy above.

I had a bachelor's dinner with Bing and his steward Cosgrove at
a pub The Ram's Head in the near town Meryton. We were
joined midway by Colonel Foster and Captain Denny of the local
militia. The military blokes are hale gents full of bluster for the
importance of their post, a bravado matched by the many bulges
pushing at their redcoats. They spend half the day striking poses
and marching, thrusting feet splayed like geese. The main street

courses with militia ranks. Denny, alluding to Bingley's willowy build, bequeathed us his routine for the development of prodigious muscles of the legs and arms. Bingley was too self-effacing to object to the officious advice, and indeed Denny was filled with the spirit of jollity rather than malice.

My black, green, brown, and blue coats might appear rather more striking were I to adopt military routines for physical maintenance, and Fitzwilliam has said that I ought to heavy up the length of my frame, lest I come to resemble a hat-rack bent double by my greatcoat in advanced years. Denny's routine is thus: find a plug of iron one stone weight; he recommended a large bar shot such as the navy launches at the rigging of enemy ships. Thrust it from waist to full upward extension twenty times. Do the same from waist to ancles by holding the arms in place and dipping the knees, keeping the muscles of the legs engaged. Next hold the iron at waist level and swivel back and forth, again twenty times. Finally, lift the iron with both hands from straight arm to bend at the breast. After each exercise is completed twenty times, repeat the whole routine between three and five times.

Foster, the elder by twenty years, insisted on the use of the lungs in addition to this muscular circuit, and recommends tying small bags full of lead shot to the ancles, then running two or three miles at a varied pace from trot to sprint. But never to run in the miasma of London – only in fresh country air. Believing all gentlemen are avid killers, Denny promised me that my hunting musket will hold steadier once I build the shoulders. As I have written the routine down, you see I do not scoff out of hand at the proposition. Cousin Fitzwm is, after all, a soldier with a brain atop his formidable body, and his taste is not utterly ruined by his rough style of life. Perhaps we'll have Bingley weighing more than the Christmas ham by the end of our visit!

Though I prefer fencing practice, I have no master to spar with me when I am away from Pemberley. Perhaps Denny will try my hand at epée when we have a fine afternoon.

On arrival at the mansion house, Netherfield, I slipped up to my bedroom with hardly time for Caroline to enumerate my perils from fatigue, the winter damp chill, and my bachelorhood – as I proceeded up the stair. Thus closed in my chamber I claim my first resting breaths today. Winter draws near and the day faded early through a furrowed brow of clouds. I shall record the remainder of today in the morning – my pen moves too slowly to keep ahead of drowsiness.

2 Nov   Netherfield Park

Continuing from yesterday. I left London mid-day upon completion of business. Pitt's new policy through Parliament requires recruiting gains in local parishes, and Gibson advised me to hire an organiser in Derbyshire. The young men have little war-lust at home, removed as they are from the scrabble of coasts and wave-ruling monarchs. I abhor the station of war-mongering my tenants; besides which every hand is needed at harvest. Pressure grows for recruits as much in the French war as the West Indies. Gibson thinks it might be done fairly with allowances distributed to recruits' families, and Pitt by policy makes it my office. Gib will run the exchanges and report back within a fortnight.

An hour before leaving Grosvenor I received a gilded letter from Lord Trawlney speaking in very open terms of his daughter's dowry, disposition, and misc. affections from the females of his family. I have shivering pondered the scene in which I would flout Aunt C's will, dismiss Anne to the top dogs of country balls, and introduce them both to a future wife who openly writes to a cousin in Australia. Yes, even that wasteland prison colony! I would needs flee Rosings to preserve my scalp.

Trawlney's expectation rests on my shoulders, for I allowed the dalliance with his daughter to be observed. Tho' I *like* the girl, I cannot love lustily with a China doll. She embodies all the best imaginings of lords and ladies lisping about female accomplishments, as her talents range from music to languages to landscape painting. In the last she has a considerable talent that might be shown in the galleries of London, but ladies' art is not treated with due respect – it is petted like a furry lap-dog by the kindest of critics, and pummeled like a badger by the cruelest. But in Miss Trawlney there is a sad lack in the art of being human. She operates as an automaton of her father's high expectations, not as a living, breathing woman. Her refinements plaster her over.

Perhaps she thinks the same of me -- the shy stiff Darcy fixed to the ballroom wall! We got on for the season by a mutual shyness and equal expectations held by society. Now my slender regard has given rise to a general expectation of a lasting attachment. What disappointment shall I cause by noticing any woman? 'Tis better to leave well enough alone, and keep myself out of debts of the heart.

The man at the inn in Meryton charged me an absurd sum at lunch to whet my lips with ale and a slice of pork pie whilst I awaited Bingley's company. My reputation precedes me. No man would be so cozening in Derbyshire -- only these day-out-of-town winches fall in line with out-held hands. Hertfordshire is between the urban and the rural spheres, and they make a business of picking pockets from gentlemen fleeing town.

So I have paid my tax. Bingley promises sprawling days of shot, country dining, and quiet. The neighborhood here is a small respectable fringe town, anyone's home, laid out among straying hedgerows and low-cupped fields. I enjoy the liberty to engage absolutely no one in discussion, particularly about war, money, soldiers, or harvests. What then? Books or music? I do not expect to meet with great conversationalists. If the larger world does not impose, what shall?

4 Nov   Netherfield

Bingley, Hurst, and I hunted pheasant this morn and brought back a brace to the cook maid. Season turns rapidly with fields leaf-littered and trees harried in cold gusts. My spirit likewise is in tumult in this northern Torrid Zone, though I cannot put a finger on the reason. Bing spoke nervously of further insurrections in Jamaica and St. Dominguez, and his concerns for two college friends dispatched to fight the wars there. Disease – yellow fever, malaria – poses greater peril than the restless slaves, he says. His friend Mayor is one of a regiment in Jamaica that lost half its men to the epidemics.

A plaintive letter from Georgiana arrived at Netherfield. The seal was broken by the time Caroline delivered it to my hands, and she protested loudly the injuries of careless post-boys. No matter. My sister seeks to buoy her spirits though quite alone at Pemberley for the winter. In addition to Mrs. Annesley's tutoring in French, Latin, and Geography, Georgie applies herself to the new compositions of the young German Beethoven, whose book of piano concertos I sent along from London last month. She says they are more challenging than any Bach or Mozart -- stirring and wild works like a musical gothic romance. Last year's misadventures have made her more than ever eager for my approval, which I constantly give with an open heart though she does not believe herself worthy. I am troubled by her loneliness and remorse. A girl of sixteen should be light in her steps and full of unsullied cheer. It is a fearful thought that she might be scarred for her formative years by that unpleasant business – that she might never trust herself again. I have not been able to keep it out of my thoughts. What more can

I do? Bring her early among the asps of London society – marry her off ere she understands her adult mind?

Our party attended a country ball this evening, an affair of little particular interest and of excessive general fluttering. Small country balls seem all the more silly and ignorant when put in contrast to the great events abroad. The country folk are little aware of French affairs and how they will soon impact us, let alone skirmishes further abroad that touch their lips as coffee and sugar. The tongues of local families hissed my income as I set foot in the room, though the figure of ten thousand pounds per annum is rather short of the mark!

In such parochial spheres, any single man with the means to maintain town and country houses must be in want of a lady to lighten his purse and keep the servants busy. I felt the pressure of every available girl pushing in like the walls of the stifling room. The punishment of dancing with a complete stranger was close at hand. Hot and close as a jungle, we were as Afric tribes, streaked in feast paint, aping smiles, lacing our dancing lines to the beat of the tum-tum. Bingley's charm quivered skirts all around us. I for my part could not find tongue to twitter with pure strangers interested only in the depth of my pockets. Caroline pronounced all that she imagines my mind to be, leaving me neither the office of charm nor of expression. I neither smirked nor curtseyed. I cut exactly the figure the whole room expected of me.

Bingley is hard and fast on a pretty young Miss Bennet, and he protested loudly when the ball came to a close and Miss B with it. She is a sweet girl. I narrowly escaped dancing with each of her eighteen sisters in the course of the evening. The Bennet mother thought it advisable to inform me, by way of her interlocutor, of the obligations of a single man of large fortune in such a scene as her daughter-filled ball, and that I was incontrovertibly a "disagreeable, horrible man" above my company. A hard fate indeed, so tactfully pronounced!

Bingley informs me their family estate is entailed, which needs must make the young ladies keen-clawed. That old tigress will not drag me to her kittens. Until one lady can advise me in corn yields, study agitator pamphlets, frame the picturesque of Derbyshire, play a lucid concerto, and present me in with the tea customs of the Orient – until she unites these talents with the grace of a pleasing person -- one woman, oh Benedick, shall not come in my grace.

Other than the letter from Georgie, I had no word from the wider world today. Bingley continues to fret over his family's part in the West Indies, and for his friends at war there. His modesty makes him culpable at every moment for the advantages he has inherited, and I am constantly advising him to think more of his *bourgeois* entitlements.

At least the introduction of young Miss Bennet lifts him from his brooding, where I remain.

5 Nov   Netherfield

Kept mostly indoors by shoddy weather, my chest of books, just arrived from London, has been my wife today. I rely on the mail-coach to transport it when I travel on horseback. It is a small mahogany chest that holds about 15 standard volumes, and I change them out whenever back at Pemberley's library. These weeks my bent runs to poetry and science, and I have in my possession old standbys – Milton, Cowper's *The Task*, Shakespeare's sonnets, a volume of sonnets by Charlotte Smith, and *Pamela*. I have just acquired from Jos. Johnson in London an odd and intriguing illuminated volume *Songs of Innocence and Experience* by a poet Wm. Blake.

Johnson may have aimed to scandalize me, but he knows I am a liberal-minded man, one who will be pleased to live the longer length of years in the nineteenth century than in the eighteenth, God willing, and he sent the book along on lending terms. The poems take the form of nursery rhymes mostly, with wallowing nude figures infused in revolutionary words with angels and innocents dragged down by a despotic system. Blake protests King, Church, and rank, and models London on Paris. I just skimmed through it today, like a boy with a picture book, but I shall read it *encore fois* with patience. The other side of my chest bends to nature: Darwin's *Botanic Garden*, Buffon's *Natural History*, Cuvier's *Revolutions*, Gilpin's *Observations* and Priestley's two volumes on Electricity.

Darwin has an energetic pen that does not scold his quatrains into perfect grace, but his lines are infused with meaning and liberal insights of science. He writes of a kind of organic evolution of forms through deep time that is quite at odds with the Bible's creation. I find it a much more compelling and creative notion than static creation, and he uses the physical evidence of the geologists to show how forms seem to have changed in time. We may all be cousins to barnacles and lowly worms – even the DeBourghs and Darcys! The French men fill my head with news of global upheaval in the deep backward of time, the time of lizards and volcanoes.

It is now fifteen years since the great Icelandic eruption that choked off summer '83 when I was a boy. I can well imagine Cuvier's revolutionary geology in our living time. The sunsets that year! The Peaks were ensanguined with the falling light from a ghastly sky, which carried a sense of cosmic foreboding so vivid to a child. My father sent a score head of sheep by ship to Iceland to help the stricken population. Cuvier seems reluctant to dissent from Biblical accounts overtly, but makes no mention of typical Creation. With my lounge at home decorated in crinoidal limestone, toadstones, and Derbyshire screws that Darcys have scavenged through the years, I have no doubt that the earth conceals more complex tales than just the sinning pair cast from the garden. My brain turns new ideas round.

Bingley and I found the leisure to walk all the gravel paths in the Netherfield vicinity at midday, and quite alone. We walked into the arboretum, and in the relative shelter of the trees we tossed a large iron pan, as the mansion house was utterly lacking in naval bar shots. Bingley purloined the pan from the kitchen, braving the wonder of the cook-maid, who has marked her new sire as an eccentric type. For what business does a gentleman have with cooking equipage? We tossed the deuced object back and forth between us, heaving it from ground to waist each time. What a pair of asses we must have appeared! Bingley tired after about fifty tosses, and left off to watch me go through Denny's routine with the great hulk heaving above my head and down to my feet. It is prodigiously heavy, a stone's weight and a half I, and it has the advantage of a handle.

Whilst I was self-conscribed to this severe labour, Bingley told me more of the state of the West Indies and his uncle's trade partner, the plantation master Abingdon. Bingley the senior nearly got in a row with an abolitionist passing out pamphlets on Bond Street last month, and his son is discountenanced by the old man's new tirades. Continuing ill news of upheaval, disease, and pointless conflict involving our men sours Bingley's taste for the coffee trade. Charles senior has great expectations for furthering the Bingley brand coffee among fashionable Londoners, and the growing manufacturing cities to the North. The practical concerns of supply vie with Bingley's deep sensitivity to injustice and wanton suffering. He will never be able to grasp the dark hand in Jamaica that prunes his coffee bushes, nor will his money ever weigh in her hands. He is equally concerned that the wars will prevent next month's shipments from arriving at Dover, and that his friend Mayor will perish beyond the Sargasso Sea.

It is five years since the great revolt, and of Pitt's 30,000 they say 14,000 have died in battle and 7,000 in pestilence. A fleet lead by Abercromby will soon be dispatched to steal Trinidad and her slaves from the Spanish, thus expanding our economy in sugar and coffee. The trade triangle rivets us on a moral crucifix.

Bingley has assigned me a valet, the young Lucent Bloom, who assisted in my toilet and advised me on the latest *vêtements de mode*. Pants are getting longer, and shoes lighter, and waist-coats simpler, and cloth in general less shiny. Embroidery is out for men. Though my wardrobe is filled with selections from two or three seasons ago, Bloom proclaimed my sartorial condition rather favourable. Nothing worse, he said, than dressing a dandy who fancies fluff and purple silks. You are a buck, sir.

We spent an eternal evening at cards, where Louisa and Caroline rehearsed all of last night's objections to the society of Hertfordshire, and Hurst bellowed about Bingley not concentrating on the game. Bingley was indeed rather diverted by his sister's reminiscences of last evening, though his complexion wore a rosier hue than the blanched powdery one of the ladies. Even I began to look on the local gathering's advantages in comparison to our limited table at Netherfield. At least Meryton's nastiness is naïve, not sentimental.

7 Nov   Netherfield

Very little to report. The country is comatose, particularly when the weather makes shooting impossible and walking unpleasant. My whole body aches from the iron pan routine of two days ago – pleasant pain that reminds me of vigorous days when as a child I dashed from home to Lambton and helped the farmers at their harvests. I renewed the ache today, with a routine in my room. Unless Caroline was at the key-hole, I laboured in privacy.

Bingley's mother and uncle, his departed father's younger brother, came down from London for the day. Upon spotting their clattering carriage in the drive, Charles joked that his mother must have prayed that God reward her with a younger substitute for her departed husband. Frank Bingley is a jolly, red-cheeked burgher, just like his elder brother was, and likewise is grown pasted o'er with the grime of business concerns. He relaxed a bit after a glass of claret and an afternoon of bird-watching in the conservatory, where the housekeeper has set up a feeder outside the window. The sun broke through for a spell. I spoke with him about wealth and the trends in coffee and tea. He has not the blind deference for landed gentry that I have come to expect from tradesmen. He said quite candidly that he finds the gentry to be mostly in Hurst's mould – the whirligig man of fashion flitting about London-town like a candy dandy – in his words. Louisa and Hurst are the archetype of the new English couple: his old name, fashion, and indulgences are paid for by her newfangled dowry. Caroline, he mentioned, has the same fat dowry and a taller, more womanly figure, besides being industrious in her training. This paltry hint I let echo off the windows without comment. He filled the silence by asking whether I might venture capital to develop Bingley brand tea from new explorations in Bengal. I prevaricated with an observation of a small brown bird that scattered the gang of woodcocks. Mrs. Bingley joined us in a shrill string of praises for the house at Netherfield, as she swooped in and perched on her husband's brother's arm. Finding me poor in information, the couple departed for a tour of the South wing.

Why am I insulted by his disdain for Hurst, when I can as clearly see the man is a worthless brandy-mop? Hurst is the nephew of my mother's second cousin, and thus a remote kin to myself.

Our lines have only recently unraveled one from the other. Perhaps I am worried that our sphere will become obsolete in the new industrial century, and we only hasten our morbidity with our lassitude. Was not the fate of the French nobility warning enough that we must remain vigorous, engaged, useful, sympathetic to the labourers?

As if Frank Bingley had read my thoughts, before leaving with his lady he requested the honour of my company in a walk around the cleaner paths out of doors. He said his curiosity had been piqued upon hearing of his eldest son's new sworn friend, the illustrious Darcy. He had known of my father, and respected him, as everyone did. He said my father represented the very best potentials of the landed gentry – to be educated, even-handed, sympathetic, and generous without guile. He said he admires his nephew's open, approving disposition, but that unfortunately that sort of character does not often make the shrewdest tradesman, however well it may do for establishment wealth. The younger Bingley's rapid, sentiment-filled actions were even less favourable in his uncle's eyes as features of a successful businessman. Finding me to be a serious and studious-seeming fellow, the uncle entreated my help, *viz.* that I might look after his nephew, and influence him towards careful thought, enduring application, and critical perception. Then perhaps I might exchange some of my seriousness for Charles's *joie de vie*, and we both emerge better in the trade. Though I could not deign to express gratitude for such unrequested advice, I bowed and let him know that I understood his meaning.

Mr. and Mrs. Bingley left in their carriage after dinner, and our party played at loo the remainder of the evening.

8 Nov   Netherfield

I have been reading Buffon, playing billiards with Bingley, and heaving about the eight-quart iron pan -- all pursuits having advantage as escapes from the sisters and Hurst. It is incredible how rapidly new money such as Bingley's adopts the high-handedness of old money – Caroline is nearly as effete as my Aunt Catherine, with none of the real respectability the DeBourgh name commands. She is fortunate to have an uncle and brother with a tolerable business sense, high energy, and abundant free labour in a coffee climate. The ill-bred behaviour of his family makes me love Charles more – he is a creature able to transcend the evils of his environment and remain rational, pleasant, and modest. At times I even envy his naïve optimism for his fellow man, when I by instinct look only to judge.

9 Nov   Netherfield

I have found an object to interest me in the country after all. Last night at a banal gathering at the family Lucas estate I encountered a most appealing creature. I thought my best chance for amusement in the country was to sift through my books, or a litter of prime hunting puppies reared on the hay field, but instead an animal woman reared in such pasture has achieved my notice.

I am disrespectful -- because I am defensive. I am unaccustomed to having a woman seize my notice without the least effort on her part. At first I marked her as she spoke with Colonel Foster, whom she stirred to a boisterous guffaw that filled the chamber. What wit could shake the beefy old soldier to such unguarded mirth? When at last we spoke directly, the minx made fun of my eaves-dropping, her eyes sparkling, and left me with a proverb "keep your breath to cool your porridge." She directly engaged in a simple and lovely rendition of Three Ravens on the pianoforte, which set me tingling despite my unperturbed air. Tho' she did not play with Georgie's precision nor Caroline's grandeur, her performance was artless melody, as the uncontemplated song of a thrush. Any lady singing of ravens who sounds like a songbird is an alchemist of the vocal arts. It suffices to say that I have never heard its equal – a natural simplicity that far exceeds the baroque monstrosities of our forebears.

Later in the evening she improved her standing further by denying my request to dance with her – a proposition that, whilst I did not seek it out, would have allowed me to study the lines of her face and form from closer range. Instead, I was left halfway across the room trying to over-listen to her bright discoursing and easy playfulness, and made half-dumb to anyone else attempting to engage me. I think, by my absent-minded "yes," Sir William Lucas believes that London society looks to me to perform the newest dances interpreted from traveler's accounts of the Abyssinian frontier.

By resisting me, she dares me to resist her. I trust, however, the infatuation will not last long -- I have recovered from the face of a pretty woman before. I shall not name her, for to name a woman is the first part towards possessing her, and our relative situations make that virtually impossible. She is confident without *hauteur*, teasing without meanness, and rational without prudishness. She represents what Wollstonecraft and Yearsley see in the improvement of the female race through education and rational conversation.

She will form an interesting counterpoint to Caroline, who has had all the advantages of wealth and society and yet has proved impermeable to application. This young lady being a kind of best-case scenario, I shall make a close study to form my own opinion on the perfectibility of the gentle sex. My anthropology of the female will pass the time in the country, at least.

As any alliance between us is absurd, considering our relative situations, I will enjoy her in theory, and claim a dance when her guard is relaxed.

12 Nov Netherfield

Cold rain has kept us indoors again today, and I have tucked into the weekly package of news from London sent by Gibson, including his year-end report on our land yields. The best news of the lot is that the harvest tally shows the estate's farms have taken in a prodigious amount this year, clearly a release from the bad harvests of '94 and '95. Though my contributions to our local Spleenhamland system kept our parish in affordable grain and potatoes during the dire years, I am relieved that the sun and rain provided for this year's boon. Nature and my tenants' hard work have carried us through. Gibson reports that Digby and Russ brought bumper bushels of tomatoes, cucumbers, eggs, pullet, and a peculiar potato with orange flesh introduced this season by Dalton, who lived for three years in the American state of Georgia. All this bounty brought to the kitchen door, and Mrs. Reynolds received it to the pantry. I imagine Mrs. Bursted whipping the potatoes into mash for the lower table; dogs gathering around the benches for a lunge at the wishbone; the energy and goodness of the staff; Georgie receiving Mrs. Reynolds' report on inventory and winterizing plans for the gardens. Bingley's servants here are not as rooted to the estate as are mine – they are hired hands, looking for any improved station that may present itself in London. Truly I miss my extended family at Pemberley.

The Times brings two points of news from America. The *Belvidere* arrived from New York with letters from 27 September informing Europe that General Washington has resigned his post as the first President of the United States. His resignation speech is printed in full, and I excerpt briefly an estimable passage: "the happiness of the people in these States, under the auspices of Liberty, may be made complete, by so careful a preservation and so prudent a use of this blessing, as will acquire to them the glory of recommending it to the applause, the affection, and adoption of every nation which is yet a stranger to it." Tho' the Colonies rebelled from us to become States, tho' they allied with the French to defeat us by sea, I yet feel that affection of which Washington speaks for liberty. We are, all of us, too conscribed in society's rules and ranks, and should revise our customs in the way of the American experiment.

Vice-president Adams, former ambassador to Britain, is expected to succeed Washington. I have great hopes for Adams's favour. I remember him speaking with my father when we were neighbors in Grosvenor Square in the '80s. He was a tart gentleman, and physically repulsive, but father believed he had a strong will and great mental powers. We must use our clout with Adams to forge stronger alliances in coming years. As vice-president he broke the congressional tie and sided with John Jay's treaty with England, and against an alliance with wartime France; though recent reports suggest squabbles between Adams and Hamilton, in which the latter advocates for American debt with the Bank of England, and the former shuns the shadow of the Union Jack.

The other news relates a live rattle-snake imported from the States, more than nine feet in length and one foot in circumference. The beast is reported as beautiful, its bite is "attended with immediate dissolution," and they may expect the fellow to be biting again soon, as they report he has not eaten since last May. Inquisitors may call on the owners in Oxford-street to satisfy their curiosity and inspect the creature closely. The major benefit of living imperially is that the whole wild world is imported to one's door step, and, rather than remaining brute forces of nature, beasts become *objects d'arte* ribbed with fantastic patterns and dashing forms. They are the caged and framed sublime, with the danger to ourselves nil. Though in a society as advanced as Britain, we become softened and delicate by not striving stridently against the wild. It is a perilous luxury.

I forwarded two adverts from the Times to Sinclair at Pemberley, asking him to select liberally from the new botanical offerings: first, of interest to my tenants, a new species of wheat from Syria that promises five hundred-to-one returns on its seeds, so prodigiously does it grow; second, for our hothouses and orchards, the Oswego Sylvan Gooseberry to make brandy, Mountain Red and White Currants, and the Florida Strawberry, with "fruit the size of a plum." Sinclair is a wizard of new cultivars and grafts, and he shall not idle the winter away.

14 Nov   Netherfield

Bing, Hurst and I took advantage of a short break in the deluge to ride to Meryton for dinner with the bulbous officers, Denny and Foster. The local militia are eager to recruit any young man who is willing to devote his body to domestic disputes, the likes of which are bound to increase in these years of penury and deprivation. Far safer to serve in England than overseas in France, Italy, Spain, or the West Indies. I am concerned their recruits may not be the best kind of police men, who must measure brute power with discipline and discretion. We endanger our liberties by placing arms in the hands of dragoons.

Denny and Foster spoke of plans to double their forces by the time they leave Hertfordshire. May they take pains to scout out worthy recruits; frankly I would rather have our English brutes sent to the international conflicts than enforce peace in domestic insurrections by way of drunken raids on demonstrators. Bad harvests, poverty, taxation, and the recent infringements on civil liberty reactionary to the French Revolution are bound to intensify the layman's conflicts with local militia. Our party also spoke of the King's recent letters of reprisal against the Spain's navy, as we are dragged unwilling into further military broils offshoot of the French aggression.

Of domestic note is our acquisition of a fever-struck young Miss Jane Bennet – Bingley's infatuation from the ball – who rode to Netherfield this dour day on more a rowing horse than a trotting one, fetched in by our ladies. By the time we returned from dinner she had fallen ill, and will stay the night. Bing has been quite useless in any other office tonight, dazed puppy.

16 Nov   Netherfield

We have hooked another fish from the floods! It is near 2am by the mantle clock, and the party is just parted. Miss Elizabeth Bennet (my object of study -- so now I have named her) came on foot -- through three miles of muck -- this morning the 15th presumably to attend her sister. Also to claim a few hours away from her mother, and in the presence of bachelors?

When the athlete entered the breakfast room attended by Howe, the whole party were adoring Louisa's new puppy bitch and I held Eliza's eye for a moment. She kept my gaze levelly, as if daring me to disapprove of her dirt. But no need, for I saw nothing of her petticoats, only her fine colour and energy. She is remarkable, I shall not deny, and I have an image of her face so inked on my mind that I feel I cannot sleep until it is translated to words. Then perhaps I can lay to rest. I am giddy. Indeed I kept up with Hurst in the wine tonight. So she is:

Not so tall, but in right proportion of limb and her air and body are light and pleasing. The fine rain brought loose auburn curls to frame her face, which is made remarkable by the intelligent expression in her fine eyes. Their colour at first appears dark, both dark and bright, but on closer inspection I found their base colour to be a deep green with a rich brown inner circumference. Her long lashes bring doubt to teazing expressions, and the curl of her lips unites innocence with experience – but what? I would guess her three and twenty, by her maturity, and yet she cannot have been much from Longbourn and the small Bennet estate.

Her words resonate in my head, even inconsequential *repartée*.

I am no longer surprised at your knowing *only* six accomplished women. I rather wonder now at you knowing *any*.

The emphasis is playful, but her meaning is deadly serious. She is a step ahead at any moment. She amuses herself with the study of female behaviour in polite society, and like me she finds it stifling. She finds lady's work silly primping for the pleasure of men, I suppose, as a follower of the Blue Stockings might, tho' she cannot have much experience of radical philosophy. Her mind would be well cultivated by serious knowledge, beyond her father's library, I mean knowledge of the world and its complexities. Caroline interprets the young lady's mean regard for feminine accomplishments as an art of male attraction, but I disagree. There is no meanness in her meaning – it is all a shrewd commentary on the state of female education.

Why am I left lonely with my conundrums when I might get rational advice from a companion? Bingley is only half a brain in such matters, and of course yields nothing by way of body. God give me a bright and rational woman – one with a heart, too, not some iron maiden in Aunt Catherine's mould, or a China doll in Miss Trawlney's, or a flounce like Caroline. The eligible women I know are vacuous. I find myself more than usual destitute of words when basking in Miss Bennet's, but my eyes stay engaged with her. My brain is flashing with visions.

To bed with me – dazed puppy! I have claimed the title from Bingley. My window faces east, and Eliza is the sun.

17 Nov   Netherfield

Despairing of any more sleep, I am up and out with my chest of books. Smith & Sowerby's botany informs me that a Bennet is common name for the wood avens (*Geum urbanum*), a name from the French for "blessed herb," thought indeed to ward off Satans from the garden. I am advised to use bennet liberally in soups and ales, and that bennet may save me from digestive complaints and halitosis. Indeed she is from a fine botanical family! Her animal family is more in doubt.

I was earlier amused by the 9th Nov. advertisement in the Times of Mr. Edward's globular nipple remedy, which has, it seems, relieved many a sore nipple in the kingdom. Though Edward guards his recipe jealously, the natural historian in me is intrigued by experimentations with herbal salves that may relieve the aches of the fairer sex. I am slipping into a perilous state of infatuation with female physic. I have not known a woman intimately these seven years; *ergo* I can hardly censure myself for lascivious thoughts.

Perversely related, I was last night put in the confusing position of having Caroline paw into my bedroom in the thick of the night. In a depth of dreams I imagined a chimney-sweep brush combing through my hair wielded by a small child-age Eliza Bennet dressed in rags, but the dream flowed away into the darkness of my room with Caroline stroking my head. This was the real world. "You are quite marooned among my bedclothes, Darcy." She cooed, still breathing the queasy claret from our evening card table. She twirled a ribbon around her finger and set the candle on the nightstand. In fact she had misled herself down the long hallway that spans the front of the house, and overshot by three doors to her left. Once I assured her that I was secure in my own bed, with my books at the side, my threads hanging in the closet, my boots by the door, and my good humour dependent upon further uninterrupted sleep, she had no rational excuse not to leave.

Down to breakfast and our guest. May her sister mend slowly!

17 Nov - continued   Netherfield

It is evening now, and I am set for bed. My heart has been in my throat all day. I feel exhausted and jittery at once. Miss Bennet is not only pretty; she is notably beautiful. We have just parted, among the others, after an evening during which I was in no command of myself, but in a kind of suspended rapture that transported me from one act to another. Happily, I did not utterly embarrass myself, and on the outside may have looked relatively composed, tho' wild the tumult within. I must keep command of my countenance. I cannot think clearly when she is anywhere close – her mere presence agitates me with the most intimate reminders of my vitality.

Morning started inauspiciously enough as her mother arrived with younger daughters in tow. Mme. believes me a snob and interprets me for the worst. Eliza held my side when I had not the words, and warmed me with food and starvation, poetry and steadfastness. She spoke teasingly of thin, slight love, and how one well-formed sonnet may starve it entirely away! I shall have to try that. Bing committed to a ball at Netherfield a fortnight hence.

I was involved in my iron pan routine near the gravel path in the topiary when I encountered Eliza an hour before supper. I bowed in severe embarrassment, and she dispersed my worry with a playful remark on how heat-tempered pans best brown the bread. She is not a mocking girl, but enjoys the humour of mischance, and I was for once not mortified to be the object of folly. I could not simply release her then, so I took her path with as much gravity as I could muster, and directed us further away from the house toward the lower meadow where we might see a deer herd in the falling light. She smilingly offered to carry the pan for me, and I duly observed that her levels of physical endurance were not to be trifled, considering her easy canter from Longbourn. I kept the pan close by my side, and wanted very much to toss the damned thing in the brush.

Her sister was feeling a little better, and might join the party later that day. I complimented her devotion, tho' I was thinking more of her talent for crossing stiles in ancle-length dress. Upon seeing a flock on the commons we engaged in a *tête-a-tête* about the virtues of sheep versus goats. She took the part of goats as the clever ones, so I obliged her with a strong bias towards the woolly sheep. She accused me of being a cruel, driving shepherd, master of a flock of mindless underlings, and I had not the words to rejoin. There was a cincture round my throat, and I was confused by the thought of her thighs moving beneath her skirts. As our talk evolved she cared not which part she had in the feud, for she could chuse a favourite young yew among her father's flock as well as a spry she-goat in the creamery shed. So peopled were our minds with sheep and goats, we saw no deer, and we went back to the house and parted in the hall to dress for supper. I deposited my heavy pan back with the bewildered cook-maid, who swept it onto the hook as though it were an ostrich feather.

My valet Bloom helped me select a new suit of an ochre colour with snug breeches and a plain silk olive vest with a white cravat to set it off. We gazed into the cheval-glass together as Bloom brushed my coat, and he asked whether the winter winds had shifted in my feelings towards Miss Bingley, or whether the visiting young lady claimed the honour of my notice. I merely demurred with a smile, and he rejoined that I was quite the lady-killer and should take care with whom-ever's delicate heart I deigned to flutter. In common with others, Bloom sees me as a stoic, tall, young, handsome, rich man, and accordingly a steel soul without vulnerabilities. I parried his inquiries by asking about the maid staff at Netherfield. Bloom proclaimed the two house maids and two cook maids to be ugly as bulldogs, but the daughter of the butler, a Miss Howe, is a beautiful bird who visits sometimes when she is not working as a governess to rich Londoners. I have recorded the name so I may engage Bloom's interests in future.

Released to supper, I chose a spot opposite on the table so I might see Elizabeth's face in full. When she sets her eyes on me, instinctively I look away to defend myself. Her look is not accusatory, but it carries a challenge. I must guard myself. For her good as well. I cannot give off too much interest that might raise impossible expectations. Her sister and Bingley are already allied in the local minds. Would that she had some worthy connexions in society – damn any fortune – I need not money! She has her own person to recommend her.

Well, to continue. Caroline positioned herself at my left, Louisa on my right, and I spent the meal sliced between sisters' wits on the subject of ladies riding next to servants in barouche boxes (Louisa – yea; Caroline – nay). My pleasure came from Eliza's wry faces and Bingley's vain endeavors to redirect the conversation towards something of general interest.

I do not always look away. I met her eyes at least a half dozen times.

The Greeks might criticize her face for slight failures in symmetry; the sisters Bingley disdain her for her independence and sartorial disarray. I am powerless but to absorb this lovely creature. She is so unlike other young women both in town and country, and what others would call imperfections are for me unique perfections that make her more alluring.

By writing a letter after dinner I tried to distract myself, and the party was quiet for the while. I wrote to Georgie about the animals in Hertfordshire and the more temperate winters in the

South. My sister the country girl loves lowing cows and a good fat pig. Alas, the zoological subject was a reminder of the pre-prandial stroll, and as soon as I looked up from my task I became hopelessly wrapped in the intercourse of Elizabeth, who is a sauce-box when you push her to perform. We had an amiable confrontation on the subject of whether fast writers are superior to slow ones, and whilst rapidity of thought is much prized by its possessor, I am doubtful as to whether fast thinkers display a superior intellect. On the contrary, I am persuaded that those who think long and deeply on subjects of importance, without any concern for precipitate action, are likely to come to the better solutions. Perhaps I was channeling Bingley the elder's request to direct his son towards serious and steady thought. Elizabeth took Bingley's part in the matter, and argued his angle much more cleverly that he himself could have done. The result of all this was that Elizabeth concluded me to be a severe and bad friend, and Bingley was reinforced in his silly ways. I did not, however, feel so much abused as aroused, and in want of more play.

In this state of suspended rapture, I found myself asking her to dance a reel on the spot as Caroline played a folk air. She pertly denied my pleasure, for a second time. For now, for now. There is a ball approaching.

What fire is in my breast!

18 Nov   Netherfield

A good morning. Before I forget my dream I must inscribe it. It was inspired by the poet Blake's allegory of the tree of knowledge, called a poison tree by him, watered with anger and tears and the fruit of it kills his enemy. In my dream I came upon Caroline weeping beneath a fig tree squeezing its trunk and twisting it as though to break it at its stoutest girth but making no advance, she rent and bruised her arms and raged distracted. A tempest accordingly raged in the sky.

I entreated Caroline to stop her assault. I wondered at the beauty of the tree's thick canopy and fine fruit hanging down to my chin, and taking a leaf between my fingers I found it to be soft hair. I dived up, as it were, into the canopy and left Caroline to break her back and will upon the iron trunk. Seated richly two score feet up the infinite tree and buffeted by the warm wind I leaned back against the trunk and saw above me, over me, who but Elizabeth closing over me, her breath stirring my hair, her arms reaching around my chest and into my pockets and then I shouted in my dream and woke to nothing but night alone to embrace me then.

18 Nov (evening)   Netherfield

Caroline taunts me with images of my mother-in-law Bennet, as a lady's imagination rapidly leaps from admiration to love, love to matrimony. I would sooner cool my porridge than inflame her raptures with a reply. And yet she is more right than she would like to believe: I have already taken three leaps from regard to infatuation. As we walked together in the paths shaded by the mansion, Caroline's pointed discourse was fortunately interrupted by the young lady in question, who was walking abroad with Louisa. I know not whether Elizabeth overheard Caroline's teasing notions, but she resisted joining the party by alluding to the width of the gravel path, which admits just three. Rather, it perfectly "frames" three figures, as Elizabeth cleverly mocked the picturesque in her denial of our company. Would I had again escaped with her to the lower meadow. Instead I was sandwiched by sisters Bingley!

In the evening gathering in the drawing room, Caroline sought the advantage of comparing her figure with Eliza's by strolling about the room. I was invited to admire the ladies, so I simply dropped my volume of Priestley and gazed at them. Indeed Caroline is a straw taller and more robust, and her gown was new and in fashion. Eliza's bears the marks of many seasons, and was wrinkled by its journey from Longbourn. But the advantage Caroline sought in physical comparison drained away as Eliza accepted the office of engaging my intellect. She teazed me brightly about my seriousness, which I tried to defend by pointing out that the central object of life is not to make a joke.

By the time I realised I was fulfilling all of her expectations regarding my pride, my resentment, and my vise-like memory for past wrongdoing, I had already been outflanked. Resistance is useless. I chose to relax, smile, and further open my senses to her sweet abuse. Her courage mounts to meet the great man she figures me to be, and I have no apologies for bearing the pride of a Darcy. She willfully misunderstands my character so as to keep her worldview intact. I cannot blame a girl, who has inherited little power in the world, for defending herself with whatever means her wits provide.

19 Nov   Netherfield

I had another explicit vision involving our innocent guest, and have grown amazed at my sleeping fancy. I am not a prude, and I like a good rollicking adventure, but I fear this one aims too close to the target. It involved me as an apothecary charged with the application of Mr. Edward's herbal nipple remedy to its prescribed region, after which my patient was most intimately beholden to me. My sudden infatuation reminds me of the weeks with Justine nearly seven years ago, when I totally lost control over my body and soul, and duly paid the price.

I shall keep steadily to my books today, and engage in no conversations but with men. I have recently become alienated from my proper self, and I shall correct the course. There is an acceptable level of interest to be allowed to exceptional females such as Miss Bennet, but my interest has gone beyond an aesthetic object of philosophy. I wish not merely to flirt with her, but to possess her – a dangerous state of infatuation.

I live in a horror of *mésalliance*, not for personal reasons, but for the lifetime of society sneering that would accompany my choice. Desire impossible to satisfy is the surest way to misery, and why would I immiserate myself and mislead a young lady whom I esteem? It is madness. I am no longer a fawning boy – I am a grown man who is expected to chuse his wife with exceptional prudence.

20 Nov   Netherfield

In order to avoid discoursing with the young lady, with whom I was left alone this morning at the breakfast table when we had returned from Sunday service, I stared a full ten minutes at the most recent logs engulphed in the hearth and teazed the fuel viciously with the poker. Then I stood as a statue at the dining room mantle. Her surprise and confusion were apparent, but I gave her no relief, I was so deeply engaged in the close observation of the chemistry of combustion. My forehead was sheened with sweat when the carriage came and I bowed to the Elizabeth and Jane Bennets' removal from Netherfield.

I am pleased to report that in my dream last night, I floated alone on an Arctic ice-burg.

21 Nov   Netherfield

Wickham, here! I am once again plagued by his presence. He was engaged on the street in flirtatious conversation with Elizabeth herself – in common with her several sisters and Captain Denny. I rode away directly, not trusting myself to hold my countenance with so taut a strain between objects of my abhorrence and my admiration.

He is come to this neighborhood in the disguise of a solider. Just as I feared, the regiments are taking on every young man looking for an allowance, and the most vapid lads are beguiled by the superficial trappings of power in dress and armament. I know not whether he has come to this neighborhood specifically to torment me further, tho' I could not assume better of him. I am more than usual kept from the society of strangers. He will prejudice them against me.

Fortunately I am off to London for the next several days, and have intensive business with Smithson as I inquire about the Demussey tracts adjacent to Lambton. I hope W does not attempt blackmail in some design to damage Georgianna's reputation.

23 Nov   Grosvenor Square, London

Gibson and Smithson met me at my club for lunch. We had a long discussion of the civic complexities of acquiring the Demussy tracts (Gibson's concern), in addition to the sheer expense of the proposition (Smithson's qualm). If we make no move in coming weeks, Demussy has promised to advertise his lands in the Times, which would almost certainly inflate the price. Always well-advised, my steward questions whether more farms and woodlands are worth buying in this time of want and adverse weather. Their possession would require greater expenditure of time on managing new tenants whose success in farming is by no means assured. The timber is valuable, but less so than it would be if it were close to a river that could bear the great beasts off to the coast where the shipyards shape them. I am averse to the notion of felling such noble tracts for mere money that I need not, as I inherited my father's instinct to preserve the natural character of the landscape.

However, there is a more modern consideration at hand, that is, the possibility that Demussy's land conceals rich stores of coal and lead. Both resources are keenly demanded as cities turn to industrialized production, and Manchester is reasonably close. Gibson proposes that we might excavate a canal from the Demussy tract all the way to the Derwent, which joins Matlock with Derby. Smithson supposed that with the financial backing of other adjacent landholders equally eager to capitalize on their holdings, and the prospects of powering the cotton industries of the county, it may well be a good investment.

Engineers are already reporting on the possibility that the river could be used to generate power to run mills along the way. The whole business makes me squeamish – I find myself liberal in social ideas, and conservative in these machinations that scar and rive the land. A tree is worth twenty quid felled and delivered to the shipyard – but what is it worth standing on my land, consorting with sun and breeze? Even when I am away in the city din, I take pleasure in recalling the noble and deep-rooted grounds of Pemberley. Smithson, the shrewd city solicitor, simpers at my sensibility.

Speaking of grounds, it will be a relief – yes, a relief! – to leave sooty London on Heeler's hoofs and reunite with the quiet of Hertfordshire. For all its inanities something draws my soul there. I hardly dare write of it. I am due back to Bingley on the 26th for his ball, and I may return early. What have I to fear from Wickham? I have all the clout, and he has only his swagger. I shall not be cowed into submission by a rakish turncoat. Besides, my acquaintance in London were informed doubtless by a spy-servant that my rooms have been lit at night. I begin to have unwanted callers to distract me from the business at hand. Gibson is off to Pemberley for the winter.

I left it with Smithson to draw up a contract that places a low bid on Demussy's tract. We shall then see how eager the family is to sell. He died leaving three children more enamoured with the

London scene than with their home in Derbyshire, so Smithson thinks they may indeed be willing to exchange land for the cash one needs to stay afloat in the fashionable world. Of course that would be a foolish financial choice unless they find a new investment to live on. Young Demussy is interested more in trade than in land management and sees his future there. They want to keep the manor for now, but the remoteness of Derbyshire might change their view. Bingley has gently asked me whether he thinks the Demussys might be interested in selling Thrushmoor Manor, which lies only thirty miles from Pemberley's East gate.

Recent word from Paris is that Malmesbury's diplomacy is stalled, or failing, though the fellow continues to try to negotiate with their republican governors. It looks as though the war will only entrench further. The Times brings ill tidings from our engagements in the South, and continual news of General Buonaparte's aggressions in Austria. This little world of England is constantly casting herself into the squalls.

27 Nov   Netherfield

Last night was the long-awaited Netherfield Ball, with the entire Meryton multitude in attendance made colourful by the regimentals, who kept the ladies light on their feet. Thus I was spared any heavy lifting in that office. The most unwelcome news of Mr. Wickham's slanders came from the lips of Elizabeth Bennet. She knew herself to be challenging my authority, and boldly did she advance, but alas her suspicions are founded on faulty information.

By asking her to dance a set early in the ball, to which she acquiesced, I knew I was opening my heart to further danger. I did not expect my reputation to follow. She hinted that I had disadvantaged Wickham by withholding his inheritance – a new spin on his perennial role as the victim. The viper has a forked tongue that slithers into the ear of any sensitive listener – my father, Georgie, and now Eliza. Wickham has confirmed the prejudices of the neighborhood by crowing about my pride, and he has propped up their pride by insisting that the great landlords are simply ranting with prejudice against the lower gentry.

Regardless of her bad information, once again I was braced and haunted by her spirit. She was the only creature in the crowded room. Though I touched not her skin directly during the dance, my hairs stood on end through the electric current in her fingers, only somewhat buffered by silken gloves. She teazed me about the formality of our conversation, which only drove me to more dogged formality. I know not how else to defend myself. This period of dizzy rapture is fated to end, I insist, because it has become entirely unsuitable for us both. She is misinformed about my behaviour with Wickham in a way I cannot possibly correct. I could change that impression only with the disarmed honesty of an ardent lover. No more am I free to marry a woman of inferior rank for love than is she to inherit a fair portion of her father's estate; we are both bound to duty in the penury of circumstance. My penury is love; hers is fortune. How might they resolve! The spectre of cousin Anne or a smart-set *débutante* from a London ballroom haunts me.

After the dance, I removed myself to the far corner of the room so I might study her undetected. I stood with my elbow propped on the mantle, beneath the great mirror, and watched her movements among her sisters, her mother, and Miss Lucas. She balanced distress with levity, laughing off absurdities all the while I saw her spirits further depressed by the weight of her circumstances. I watched and absorbed her, then turned towards the mirror and closed my eyes to imprint, as acids on a copper plate, her form on my imagination.

I am in love with her. I doubted it before, I thought it only a passing fancy, but everything points to a deeper affliction. She permeates my imagination, she boggles my reason, she masters my self-command. Her pull is gravity itself. It is time to break, and save myself.

Well well, of the dance otherwise: Bingley is presumed by the neighborhood to be soon engaged to Jane Bennet, and indeed he is characteristically incautious with his affections. The Bennet mother was piping the too-soon news to her great rivals in the room, and her younger daughters were left free to claim undue notice by insipid loud talk and buffoonery at the pianoforte. The youngest banged on the instrument at the far end of the room whilst Bingley's country quintet were still in full swing. I was openly disgusted – equally by my blackened reputation at the hands of Wickham, by my pollution in Eliza's eyes, and by her whole family's behaviour. Other than the few moments I held her attention, it was a bleak evening indeed. She seemed to share my sentiment, for she looked purely miserable throughout the latter half of the dance.

Longbourn is set to be inherited by a cousin Collins, who was in attendance last night. He singled out Eliza with his officious attention, implying that he aims to claim her. Collins is a blowsy, foolish bloke, an obsequious milksop in a clergyman's collar. He ceremoniously informed me that my own Aunt Catherine is his benefactress. Ah, injustice! The only thoughts that bring me consolation are that should Eliza feel obliged to accept him, she will not be destitute, and that I may betimes share her company when she settles at Hunsford on my Aunt's estate. What conversations might we have in the corner of the room whilst we leave the DeBourghs and Collins to suffer one another? What further intercourse might we have in that intimate situation? Driven thus to a stone-cold married life with Anne, am I an honourable man? Would my selfish desire justify dishonouring her? Nay – there is no future with her except through marriage, and such an alliance is nearly impossible. Nearly – she is a gentleman's daughter, but – I am not a man who acts rashly. I must shun the *mésalliance*.

Damn. I bring this suffering upon myself merely by caring what she thinks of me and engaging in idle speculation. I draw alternatively on fantasy and horror! I must check my novel reading – Richardson is polluting my mind. There is no way for this to end well – there is only the near distraction of London for the Christmas season. I am impatient to regain mastery of myself and my reputation.

I wonder whether Wickham will attempt some blackmail before the party retreats. I shall hasten our removal. She shall be forgot once we are forced asunder.

28 Nov   Netherfield

I was not fifteen minutes into my morning walk, nearing the edge of the park, thinking over the recent evenings and my wild infatuation, when suddenly Wickham in full regalia and sword rode up on a charger and accosted me with a tart good morning. I deigned to touch my brim and chose the other direction to proceed. Wickham, still on his horse, turned beside me and agitated him with conflicted reigns till the beast snorted and stamped. He then saucily inquired after my sister. I replied that Georgie is well and safe, and bid him good morning. He rode ahead in my path, and turning his horse sneered:

"You deprived me of a precious wife. Who is your love that I may meddle withal?"

This having no answer I turned again directly back to Netherfield and he off towards Meryton. Could he have an idea of my regard for Eliza Bennet? Would his fellow officers have told him of my dancing with her the other night? At least he uttered no direct demands on my pocket-book. He will find a way to turn Georgie's indiscretion to his advantage once again. I have warned Gibson and Fitzwm about Wickham's intrusions by letter today.

We must leave this perilous place.

2 December   Grosvenor Square, London

I am returned to the city zoo and locked in my library cage. Though I generally use my influence over Bingley for only friendly ends, I am a little ashamed of our precipitous quitting of Netherfield. With the whole county in expectation of Bingley's union with Jane Bennet, Caroline and I told him that his alliance was not wise, though for different reasons. Caroline is determined for her brother to marry a woman of fortune so they may inflate the Bingley stock. She even has the temerity to mention Georgie as his match, which makes both me and her brother squeamish. I, on the other hand, care little about the Bingley wealth, but I do care about my friend's feelings, and I voiced my concern that Miss Bennet seemed pleasantly indifferent to Bingley's attentions.

I am not perfectly satisfied as to whether my reading of her face as untouched by love was intentional to serve my own desires. If Bingley married Miss Bennet, her sister would be often in our company, and I am helpless to resist her. Especially with the involvement of Wickham in Eliza's prejudice against me, I am on quaking ground. It is better to steer clear of all. I am uncomfortable, though, with manipulating Bingley to assure my own austerity.

We shall see whether London can serve him up a distraction wrapped in muslin and lace.

5 Dec   Grosvenor Sq.

Just returned after a late evening at Drury Lane, where I took
Bingley to see Kemble at Hamlet. Stunning performance.
Bingley's eyes were wet at Ophelia's madness and the
denouement, but I was most captured by Kemble at the moment
where he bids that his "too too solid flesh would melt," and
figures the globe as a rank garden gone to seed. Flat, stale,
weary, unprofitable. Man delights him not, nor woman either.
Would that it were so!

Were not Bingley and I a swag pair of bachelors about town!
Pockets lined with riches, toast of the grandest city on Earth, and
both sobbing into our sleeves over the lamentations of the Bard
and two lost country maids. Well well. It is a tragedy, made
alive by our great men of the stage, and none better than Kemble.
The loss of our hero's hope alongside the drowning of his mad
love chilled the marrow of us both.

My carriage left Bingley staring on the curb at Russell Sq., and I
drained a glass of claret at my club before returning quite alone
to my darkened rooms. Next time we go to theatre it shall be
something silly and sinful of my parent's generation – *She
Stoops to Conquer* would do. Marlowe can teach me how to flirt
with saucy barmaids; Hamlet can only teach me hate my own
cowardice.

The rest is silence – for today.

6 Dec   Grosvenor Sq.

Pitt triumphed over the rancour of his critics this week by
pushing through his scheme for raising capital for the war with
France from the Parliamentary committee of Supply, Ways, and
Means. We landed gentlemen are his usurers. Some starchy
Tories have branded the bill a damp squib, but some eight

million pounds sterling we gentry have pledged already, expecting returns in the five percents for a three-year period. Gibson anticipated my agreement with the scheme and had Smithson prepare fifteen thousand of my liquid assets to be invested in the patriotic scheme, which nevertheless promises remuneration.

The editors at the Times agree with my gentleman's sense of burthen: "men of property should come forward to the assistance of Government by voluntary contributions, and supply those wants which must otherwise be satisfied by imposing new burthens on the lower orders of the people. Motives the most powerful and decisive call on them to display this generous and dignified patriotism." I have no sons or brothers at war – the best I can lend is my gold to our cause. The money has lain darkling in a bank vault since my father died five years ago – let it work!

Today Sir Trawlney marched across May Fair to my house, and boldly interrogated me on my interest in his daughter who, it seems, has several suitors among the London set. I demurred directly, and am relieved to be relieved of any expectation on that front. He has crossed me off his list! He is a high-bred jade used to getting his way, and I believe I rather affronted him with my directness. Great men must brook disappointment as well as small ones; besides, he and his daughter see in me only a manor house, snug farms, and a fat cheque-book. They look not for a companion, a father, a loving husband, and an intellect to discourse at dinner. Adieu.

Also Caroline called in the evening to ask me openly about my feelings for her. It seems she thought our hasty retreat from Netherfield -- and our joining forces against Jane Bennet -- signaled a shift in my wishes. Though superficial in many ways, Caroline is a shrewd woman in the business of marriages, and she looks to have a stellar season in London if I am not to be hooked. She wilted and cried when I disavowed any intentions towards her. How can my conduct have given rise to any expectations? I exert myself to behave with such reserve as to give no improper hope to ladies, but alas, their own hopes form false impressions. Fortunately, once she recovered, we parted friends, and she asked me thrice to send her love to Georgie, and to keep some of it for myself.

That's two eligible ladies repelled in one day. Shall I take up a collection of hair-locks of the overthrown, like a murderous Gothic viscount?

What must Elizabeth think of me, leaving her neighborhood with no explanation, and after our many encounters? I would give ten quid to know her thoughts this moment. Is she disappointed? Is she out of doors, or in the library? Does she practice her playing, or is she reading? Is Wickham still stealing moments with her? Has her fat cousin claimed her as his bride? I have as yet resisted the temptation to engage a spy.

Wickham, usurper of Hertfordshire! My heart's fooled sure.

8 Dec   Grosvenor Sq.

Smithson returned news from the Demussey family that they have requested three months to consider my offer for their land, at which time we will reconvene. Into my hand on Great Russell Street was thrust a pamphlet about land in America, expansive and wild tracts full of possibility. America has filled my head since my earliest memories of their war for independence, when my father lamented the violence committed under the command his old friend, Thomas Gage, in Lexington and Concord. My father told me then that the sword of the parent ought never be darkened with the child's blood. Though I was only seven years old I remember it as yesterday, my father ranting in the library as he read the month-old dispatches from the Massachusetts colony.

My imagination runs wild with visions of what it would be like to shed off all this chalky custom and make a break for the New World. There, my money would go even further and my title would not obviate ninety-nine of one hundred women. I might marry as I chuse. But at what sacrifice? I should have to assure Georgie's happiness in marriage before I could consider emigrating. And what of my home, my country, my king?

Pitt's scheme to raise funds for the wars has ended with some eighteen millions sterling pledged – and the Times reports they had to beat men back from Parliament's door to close the proceedings. My fifteen thousand are beans in the cauldron.

Frank Bingley yesterday took a large risk at the India House by engaging the ship *Abergavenny*, under Captain Wardsworth's command, on a set of trade missions with Bombay and China. The West Indian wars and the slave question have so far stressed his son's dedication to business that the uncle has gone into speculative trade in tea and spices with the East. Bingley came to me today with the broadest grin to grace his face since the Netherfield Ball. I ordered five-pound satchels of his finest oolong, cayenne, and curry, and I sincerely hope they will flavour my table at Grosvenor by New Year's next. In addition to trade in the East Indies, Charles has lit upon dark Africa as the future of imperial strength; though he had not spoken two minutes together about coffee in the mountains of Abyssinia before he moved on to the prospects of whaling and competition with the American Nantucket men for the riches of spermaceti and ambergris. I had no voice in this matter but to encourage his steady application to one or other of these divers endeavours, rather than thrash through them all at once.

I have engaged Bloom to continue as my valet in London. Sutton sent him out into the markets to buy me an eight-quart pan, or a large bar shot, whichever he discovered first. It was a roar to see the slender lad limp up the marble steps with the pan in hand, crowing all the way about his besotted leather shoes. I thanked his labours with a Crown, and he was back in humour by dressing time before dinner. He continues to have a crush on Bingley's butler's daughter, Miss Howe, who is governess to the Rimpledons in St. James's Square. Bloom loves the secresy they must keep, in light of her sensitive position.

Methinks he sees her only in public, only in the daytime, and only from a distance of twenty yards because she is unaware that she has an admirer. I advised Bloom to leave off stalking harts like Miss Howe and set a snare for some gamey rabbit.

11 Dec   Grosvenor Sq.

I am in a peevish state, thrown from exstasy to despair by the commerce of my imagination. I have seldom felt more miserable. Why should my inclination chuse a woman who is impossible for me? What perverse torture have my heart and brain arranged for one another! If my body were the kingdom itself, England would be rattled in earthquakes, volcanoes, and tempests. All this riot, and I have not even seen the lady for a fortnight!

I feel uncomfortable with Bingley, who despite his light nature and good news in trade is still brooding over Jane Bennet. How cruel it would be to purge my heart to him about the sister of his own affections! Yet I long to confess to someone my agony. Merely to speak on the matter might free me! Shall I become a papist, and confess to my priest?

My iron pan, and the company of men, business, and talk of war have been my best strategies. News has recently arrived to

London that Empress Catherine of Russia died on the 17th of November – a day when I was first infatuated with the young lady from Hertfordshire. We shall have to see whether that vast, cold dominion can be ruled by the untested hand of Czar Paul I, for he is unlikely to have the iron will and genius of his mother. She was a great torch of the Enlightenment, with her German origins and generous mind for science and politics. The article in the Times surveyed her many pursuits, her correspondence with Voltaire and Diderot, and her doctrine of monarchal benevolence that we in England would be wise to follow, lest our rulers end up in the French way.

The gentlemen of London continue to besmirch her legacy with fantastic tales of her sexual appetites, and little else has filled the smoking rooms this week. Smoke and sex have filled my dreams as well, though only half-remembered and too vague to set down here. Frustrated love is an agent of copious wine, and I am a Silenus.

12 Dec   Grosvenor Sq.

If it be only a slight, thin sort of inclination, one good sonnet will starve it entirely away.

In dreams, when I am most at liberty
to grieve, resist, ache, rekindle, and feed
those wishes now unfolded from the seed,
in lucid dreams the sun unfurls the weed.
She is that weed, her verdure fills my brain,
a wilderness bedazzles where I gaze,
her voice a breeze, her form a leafy maze,
each night her subtle vine enfolds my pain.
My sleeping self is revolutionary:
He splinters custom's tree to kindle fire,
now primitive, I dance and stomp the beat,

the rhythm of a starving visionary.
My family name is smoking on the pyre,
as oak to ashes goes, I climax in defeat.

Starve, damn you. It is too racy to share, but it is true to my
mind. It seems like two poems in one, with the octave and the
sestet pulling away from one another. I require a volta, where I
must shift my images and come back changed upon the ground
of the octave. And so it is: her wild nature turns savage my
desiring mind. Perhaps if I actively figure her as an underling, a
weed, a pest, an unworthy, she will have less command over my
regard -- diminution by metaphor.

I fear I am not among the English poets. Nor starves my desire!

14 Dec   Grosvenor Square

This morning Aunt Catherine arrived to her house in Cavendish
Square with only two hours' notice for her housekeeper. She
came alone but for a lady's maid, a footman, and her personal
French chef – but without Anne. She assures me that Anne
needs no exposure to the public eye by way of coming out, and
that her complexion is better served in the Rosings conservatory
than in the saloons of London. Vowing to whip the winter
season into a soufflé, I suppose, as a course to precede the
wedding cake she's long been baking – my Aunt came almost
immediately to my rooms, her Cleveland Bays still frothing in
the street, and accosted me.

She wondered what a virtuous young man would do in town
during the Christmas season, which is good only for vice-filled
balls and indulgent purchases for unworthy friends and relations.
She amazed how I was such a stranger to her house in Kent, and
what I could have been doing in Hertfordshire. I shrink to
mention Bingley, whose virtues as a human do not counteract

her distaste for the mode of his wealth, and his sisters' upstart presumptions. When she deduced I had spent weeks in Hertfordshire in their company, she supposed Charles was infecting me with the seditious notions of Ogilvie, Paine, and even Thomas Spence; reformers whom, it seems, ought to be drawn and quartered on the north terrace of Windsor for their ungodly critiques of established wealth. I privately amused that Bingley's own uncle had so recently been praising the Tory prattling of Bolingbroke, when I, her very blood nephew, am more likely to support reforms of Paine's design.

She resolves to accompany me to social engagements, and put up a strong front in the onslaught of Darcy-DeBourgh as the most exclusive brand of gentry. I am to be groomed for my proper seat in the House of Commons, she claims, so as to scatter the whirligig aspirations of tradesmen and manufacturers who aspire towards governance.

Her demands are not only of a political nature. Anne's age, twenty-four, is quite perfect for the production of a first child, and she is eager in the business of securing a stud. She means to force me into this marriage within the year. She is not a woman to be trifled with, I well know, and yet I feel more by the day the despotism of this system that would stifle true affection for the amassing of wealth in cloistered and exclusive families. Am I to emulate her, to marry my cousin and resign myself to a long adulthood of mere filial tolerance surrounded by servants disciplined only by fear and sycophancy? Are my children to be sickly in-breeds? How am I to manufacture passion for my cousin? Am I to torture my imagination into moulding her as a woman pleasing to my senses and mind together?

Anne's father, little I knew him, was a severe landlord whose main business in life was to squeeze the ambergris from his tenants to sell in the marketplace. Poor Anne! With a father like a juggernaut and a mother hell-bent to demonstrate her inherent superiority of rank, but with little real information or cleverness to mediate that severe prejudice! At least I and Georgie had liberal parents who wielded their power with mercy and whose affection for each other went beyond dowry and title. Would I actually move backwards in time, back into the *ancien regime* mindset, in this era when we have a new century and a new equality to foster? I recall the disdain of Hertfordshire families who assumed just this of me. Were I a French D'arcy of such ilk I would find my head dissevered in a basket.

With that strange blend of family flattery and bald admonition, my Aunt addresses me as though her will is mine. On that happy date of her planning she would have the next two generations of our family under her sceptre. I am immersed in the awful image of the dowager Catherine presiding over Pemberley and my own children. She will have a fountain with neoclassical nudes spouting from the front run, even before she has a grandchild to indoctrinate. It is little wonder first sons of wealth take to hunting, drink, and mistresses – all blessed escapes from their mothers-in-law. Shall I marry as I am expected, and take a lover among the more comely of the lower classes? I would hate myself.

In true first son character, then, I begged leave from my Aunt after supper to attend to important business in my library, that is, the Fox & Hound on the East End. I adopted the name of a modest Mr. Benson from Surry, and appeared at the pub in my brown coat and derby. Increasingly I find an alias to be a welcome refuge. The East Enders share their ale over real problems, actual travails and hardships of working men. Such hardships we face as a country – famine, lack of work, wars, taxation, disease, poverty – all is forgot in the silly self-obsession of gilded ballrooms. The more I see of the world, the more I am dissatisfied with it. I have no one to confide in.

In going out late I missed the note from Caroline calling me to their whist table, and assuring me her brother is still a puddle of sap. But for reasons more substantial than heart-ache. Bingley received news that his friend Mayor – fighting now under the command of Captains Collingwood and Gott in St. Dominguez – has died on his ship, which was blown up on 14 October. He is buried in that sultry Caribbean sea. I never met the man, but Bingley's ardent friendship with him, his praise of Mayor's open affections and studious learning at college, painted me a vivid picture of the loss to our circle in his death. I remember Bingley saying that, excepting myself, he had never met with such a clever fellow. Adding to his lament is the fact that Mayor was not born with the silver spoon (as was I), and thus his wife and two children are destitute. We send off our most meretricious men to pointless wars fought over immoral business. Bingley believed his friend had a great future in engineering – turnpike building, I think. I have sent immediately my condolences and will visit at Russell Square in the morning to support him in what ways I can.

Caroline also informs me by letter that Miss Jane Bennet has announced her arrival in London for the season, though she is bound to different circles than our own and made no mention of any sisters joining her. She stays in Gracechurch Street with an uncle. Caroline presses me to keep this intelligence secret from her brother. I have no objection to select secrecy, especially where it aids in my own self-possession. I must guard me from that zone of danger. But oh – the temptation to dive back into sweet madness!

To chasten myself I went alone to Macbeth at Drury, with Kemble at the lead and Mrs. Siddons cutting a wonderful weird Lady Macbeth. I do adore Shakespeare's lunatic women. Kemble plays a new lead almost every night, and I am amazed at the capacious drawers of his mind. His Macbeth was shaking with murder and remorse right up to the point where his head ensanguined the stake. I found a perverse satisfaction in the tragedy's inevitable recourse to death.

17 Dec   Grosvenor Sq.

Bingley and I went out walking around Bloomsbury, a lively neighborhood with an open market and wholesale construction of new houses. The Bingley house is one of the first to have been completed in Russell Square, and the foundations of several more residences on the east side is incipient to the continuance of development in that quarter. Bingley and I walked away from the groans of workmen and mules, and found relative repose in Bloomsbury Square, though today, chilly and damp, was not friendly to the idle bench-sitter.

The sad news of Mayor brought out Bingley's best qualities. He was filled to the brim with celebratory sorrow for the fellow, and used the spirit of his lost friend as a buoy for his own spirits. Rather than slipping into despond, Bingley's eyes were filled with grateful tears for the gift of his friendship, and the hope that his passing is a release from the trials of this life. I sat listening whilst Bingley recited his favourite tales of their college days, Mayor's steady application to his studies, and his equal devotion to happy mischief and jolly adventure. At Oxford the lads once dressed the marble statue of Sir George Cooke in a wild-patterned Indian pai-jamah like a Sultan, and topped his cold Grecian column with a smoking pipe of opium. Serves him right, the deuced Tory -- the marble man needed a bit of loosening up!

Mayor jotted a sketch of the scene with Bingley presenting the pipe to the marble Cooke, and later he painted it finely in oils. Bingley keeps the evidence of the crime hanging in his bed-room at Russell Square, and says his mother still laughs heartily upon seeing it. I visited it myself before parting with Bingley, and found much to praise in the Oriental interpretation of the doughty faux-Grecian. Our artists must move beyond Greece, truly to know the world.

Caroline joined us in the parlour for lunch, where she winked at me every time her brother looked down to his plate, so eager is she to be in my confidence, and to keep Jane Bennet's arrival a secret. I am tempted to reveal her location, as it would bring Bingley some deserved cheer, but also I am the coward who shrinks from that family like a guilty ghost. She whispered with flirtatious desperation in the hall as I retreated and, other than a look askance by the butler, we communicated our silence undetected. Bingley's mind may stay with Mayor.

I spent the remainder of the day at my club. Most of the political talk surrounds the death of Catherine of Russia and auguries of what may follow in the vacuum of her leadership. Britain is in pursuit of the Treaty of Triple Alliance, in which Russia's powers in the negotiations for peace are indispensable, and the political men believe that Turkey, Denmark, and Sweden will flee the yoke of Russia now that Catherine's fist is un-seized, which strongly alters prospects for the Treaty. The new Emperor, son of Catherine, is said to be of very moderate faculties and an unfavourably heavy character. His first dictate from the throne was to order a funeral for both of his parents, his father being dead these four and thirty years. With such gazes into the backward abysm of time, observers wonder whether the man is capable of ruling Russia in the time of France's aggression. Buonaparte's victories and defeats fill the papers, and though he meets both victory and defeat in his campaigns on the Continent, he yet goes on, and on, and on, claiming with his grandiose tongue the lands that often thereafter fall to his sword.

18 Dec   Marylebone Park, London

It is the purist of winter days, bright, shining, free. Snow reflects the liquid sun and softens the lines of every thing. Bingley recruited me here for hunting, but I received word that he is held in business with his uncle, so I'm left to myself and see no joy in shot-through birds. Thankfully Hurst is out of it too. Also I missed Aunt Catherine's daily commandments letter by a few steps (out the servant's back door), so it lies unopened somewhere amid the city din. I've brought my journal (you see) and boots built strong enough to tromp down the River Ness monster.

I shall walk.

Natural light recovers me after so many days and nights in rooms, astride fires, living only as a series of vague impressions scattered across eon evenings. The king's health, the prince's paunch, militia unrest, America's liberty, slave revolts, slave qualms, the price of cotton, sugar, indigo, coffee, tea, mahogany, cocoa, pepper, fallen women, the education of women, the Grand Tour, sunburnt squares in Sicily, land taxes at four shillings to the pound, the new poetry, negroes free in England, property, status, sycophancy, wine-breathing, strutting, observing and concealing. Life is a string of parrots sniping and pecking each other's fairest feathers.

Elizabeth Bennet. She is my torment and refuge; thoughts of her are the parts of me I hold close. It is a game I have come to play during the last week, so I can set rules on what would otherwise make me mad. When she appears to me, I greet her with gentlemanly reserve and pointedly ask her to leave the environs of my brain, as she is trespassing. I then engage intensively in some other activity for the day, preferably loaded with numbers to remember and precise wordings (natural science and business especially) until I am exhausted, and then I engage a friend (Mr. Sweeney gossips sublimely) to discuss the minutiae of sartorial trends at court over a flagon of claret until it is time to collapse in bed.

Only then fall the locks on my brain's casements and so she sweeps in. The apparitions are quite unchaste; I sometimes wake amazed at my innovations and so sets in the next day of stained images I must attempt to bar from my notice. I am more alive asleep, and dead discoursing; I am more awake in dreams, and sleep walking daily; I am grown inattentive to women. I am like the Kongo zombi, slave to the magician she, but instead of lacking a soul she has given me one. Rather she has lent me one, but she owns it still.

You see, diary, why I try to keep busy daytimes.

Fitzwm will come to-morrow from his father's estate in Yorkshire, and has sent ahead a letter that he must urgently speak with me.

Though I came to the park mid-day, the sun is falling fast and the cold at its back. I shall return to the evening climate of a hot drawing room. Thankfully our host is devoted to good Burgundies. If I do not soon find more to occupy my time than politics, gossip, and wine, I shall become Prince Regent.

19 Dec   Grosvenor Sq.

Cousin Fitzwm arrived this morning in a flush, and Bloom had hardly a moment to bring in his trunk before my cousin ushered me to the lounge and had out with his business. He received a letter at Gravesbrook via an unknown messenger – the missive was left wedged in the front door – but its author was soon recognised. He has at last heard from his old comrade-at-arms, Henry Bayard, who has been in France since the fall of the Bastille. Fitzwm recalled for me the whole of his tale, how Bayard was a decorated young officer and intimate friend and mentor of the young enlistee (Fitzwm was hardly eighteen when he went into service), and besides from a very respectable family and intended to be heir to a considerable fortune. When news came of the uprising in 1789, Bayard practically dived into the Channel, so eager was he to witness the spectacle and learn from its events how such reforms might be imported to our country. He was gone within a week.

For many months his superiors in the army and his family held out hope that he would soon return, and not need to be reprimanded or worse (as became the case) marked as a deserter with a price for his apprehension. It seemed no plea from friend or family could locate him in the new fervour of that emancipated land, let alone bring him back, and at long last his position both as soldier and heir was given to another. His despairing father disowned him and passed his inheritance to a younger brother, without being able to inform him of his unseating. Fitzwm, his closest friend, received a single letter a year later telling him that Bayard had fallen in love with a French woman, and would not return to his old life in the land of crowned despots. So callous were his actions, Fitzwm knew not what to make of it. Fitzwm did inform Bayard's family, however, after which was soon accomplished the business of disinheriting their eldest.

Time passed and never another word from him, until last week. He is alive in Paris, but very far gone with consumption. He has begged Fitzwm to journey to France in haste to discuss his final arrangements and try to make some amends. There is a more particular matter than the dressing of old wounds: Henry is the father of two young sons, who will become orphans upon his death. Their mother, it seems, passed away within the last year of consumption, and Henry is rightly afraid of the miasma surrounding his Parisian home. The letter contained no other details but an address in an unsavoury part of Paris, and a timeline – Henry expects to live for another month, but probably not more. He is quite destitute.

Fitzwm dispatched a letter to the Bayards conveying this intelligence, then rode in haste to Grosvenor to beg my advice. Not merely advice – he has also to ask me to join him on the adventure, should we be able to secure safe passage. It is by no means easy to travel in these days of looming war, but Fitzwm believes his military connexions may provide. I asked to think it over for the afternoon, and by early evening I had acquiesced.

After all, what have I to keep me here? A rabid Aunt, the nattering sister of a friend, a city full of gossips and hen-peckers, and dark dirty days that brood over me one after another. The French adage -- *la tristesse est la maladie du charbon Anglois* – this is my life. Coal-burnt sadness besotted with frustration – that is the English way. Fitzwm has been out all evening seeking our passage across the Channel, a precarious business in this time of war.

22 Dec   Grosvenor Square

It is the darkest day of the year. The lamplighters come by three to illuminate the streets in dusky flames, streets made ever darker by the collusion of winter, clouds, and the foul breath of factories. It seems every week brings a new copse of chimneys to London, and to batter out the cold every house exhales effluvia. We keep to wood on the West End, a better smelling and burning fuel than coal, but the turbulent winter makes a common misery of the atmosphere in the bowl of London-town, dark as devils. Perhaps my mood affects the squalour as well.

I feel I must escape to the peace of Derbyshire, or to the broil of France. But the season requires me to make my London rounds to close business for the year. In a few days, after Christmas, perhaps I may escape. There is no certain news about a passage to France, but Fitzwm works the matter day and night. I have hardly seen him at Grosvenor since he arrived in town.

Taking my weekly passage through Mr. Johnson's bookshop at St. Paul's Churchyard, I returned the lent copy of Blake's *Songs of Innocence and Experience*, and Johnson pressed into my hands his more recent work, entitled *The Marriage of Heaven and Hell*. It looks as perverse and intriguing as the first, perhaps more. Also I had the pleasure of meeting an infamous author of our times, a radical and adventurous rapier of the pen in full belief of the future perfection of man and of his present destitution, Mr. William Godwin, who I at first took as one of Johnson's Unitarian friends. Upon hearing that I was none other than a land-endowed gentleman, the very scarecrow for his spears, he hastily pumped my hand and entreated me to read his novel, which is it seems, a distillation of the treatise on Political Justice that made the rounds among workers a few years ago. Before I even had a chance to celebrate my fondness for long, melodramatic novels, he had pressed a copy of it into my hands with a hearty "Merry Christmas, my dear son of fortune!"

Despite his odd aspect, I liked his confidence. Even a great critic of the English hierarchy still sees the lords as human beings beneath the velvet. Surely Johnson's friendship encouraged him to believe he might find in me a sympathetic ear. And of course, his scandalous history with Mary Wollstonecraft adds to my intrigue about these leading intellects of radical London. I wouldn't for the world share my days with the old crust such as Aunt Catherine, but I believe the younger set, those wealthy in trade, progressive like cousin Fitzwm, will be amused by my *petit rencontre* with Godwin.

Well, to the novel. I have read it rapidly over the course of two days. It is called *Caleb Williams* after its hero, a young strapping commoner disfavoured by falling into the favour of a capricious nobleman, a Mr. Falkland. Caleb is too curious for his class. From a critic's perspective on fine literature, the book is a mere gothic melodrama not far removed from Radcliffe, full of chases, fires, rescues, escapes, chests of secrets, and long-winded exclamations. Triumph and tragedy come in the same breath for our young Caleb. He is English, but must fall into the aliases of Irishman, Jew, and crippled monstrosity, as his person is under constant persecution from the ephemeral but indelible Falkland, the local squire. They are mutually obsessed; smitten even.

For all its silly monologues on the valiance and caprice of the landholding gentry, as a political protest to legal oppression, it is a work worth bearing in mind. I well know the absolute power of law I hold over my tenants, despite living after the Magna Carta, in an era where laws are said to protect men equally, it is certes not so. If I chose to ruin a tenant or peasant it would take a matter of seconds, executed by my choice of voice or pen. I have seen it done many times. A few years before I came into inheritance, I recall my father lamenting Aunt Catherine's vindictive cutting off of tenants if she disapproved of any detail. In '78 she broke contract with a tenant who she learned to have had a Catholic mother – of all prejudiced and small minded actions reactionary to Catholic relief – and unceremoniously de-roofed them and set them loose in mid-Winter on the Kentish coast. My boy's mind immediately pictured a raving Lear wandering Dover's heights, though I know nothing of the aspect, age, or family of this unfortunate man.

Father taught me that tenants are in charge of their own affairs, and are entitled to the respect of independent men with free choice to prosper or flounder. They are to be aided when plagued by uncontrollable circumstance, as they have not the means to recover to their former state like we do. Reputation is equally important for lord and tenant, and discretion dictates wise judgment before any public censure. Still, Godwin's work, though imperfect in many ways, reminded me that my tendency towards appearing above my company, when among strangers, is unbecoming of the gentry. Elizabeth mocked me for that. I shall have to learn from her wisdom, too, and press myself to being affable more widely.

Like Blake, Godwin claims that the men themselves are not inherently evil, but the institution of reputation and prejudice, backed by unequal distribution of legal redress, is the source of corruption. The hero Williams gains improper knowledge by learning Falkland's guilty secret, and once in possession of this chest of horrors, he cannot escape the desperate revenge of his formerly beloved lord. Williams is entrapped inside a network of prisons – physical, of course, which is easily overcome with rough tools, but once this is broke he finds himself incarcerated in a prison of reputation, and his lord vows to keep him within the borders of England, Scotland, and Wales, eternally spat upon and maligned.

The prison is the ideology that one man cannot stand up against another with equal eyes of the law, unless they hold the same rank. Justice in the Kingdom of England has long torn off her blindfold.

23 Dec   Grosvenor Sq.

With Eliza's image still haunting my dreams I could not resist a trip by carriage to Gracechurch Street, where her sister is wintering with the Bennet relations in Cheapside. I know not clearly what I wanted from exposure to Jane Bennet – perhaps a glimpse of a face so nearly related to her. Perhaps only to pass some idle time with an object of curiosity. I would never have been so determined about concealing Miss Bennet's being in town were it not for Caroline's leading the way, and now I rather regret that we spent weeks in close proximity without renewing the acquaintance. I have shaken off any sense of danger in this renewal – I am quite beyond the squeamishness I felt in those last days in Hertfordshire. I am hungry. If I am not to be complete master of myself, I may as well surrender to my passion rather than the expectations of ladies whose interests end with my purse. I have given too much deference to Aunt Catherine, Caroline, and my own sense of self-importance as it is.

So, I dismissed the carriage a few blocks away and set up a vigil at the corner, whilst also window-shopping and inquiring about trade in this scruffy neighborhood. Like the East End pubs and piers, Cheapside circulates the breath of working men, the rise and fall of fortunes, friends and trade rivals. A few mangy urchins fingered my greatcoat, and I dispersed them with a sprinkling of coppers. Before long I saw Miss Bennet emerge with an elder woman on the street, and the pair proceeded to local shops to procure meat and wine for the feast. Jane Bennet is a remarkably lovely girl, utterly symmetrical and demure, and her face is made more poignant by the tinge of melancholy I discerned at her lips. She is I think more beautiful than her sister, but she is *il penseroso* to her sister's *l'allegro*. She is naïve and weighed upon by disappointment – how else could she be by her limited education – whereas Eliza is spirited and defiant despite her modest means.

I followed Jane and her escort for the better part of an hour, my chin tucked within my collar and my eyes searching just below my brim. The ladies acquired a handsome but reasonable feast for their holiday table, including a parcel of candied apples for the children. Alas, when a wine merchant engaged me in a debate about Burgundy versus Barbarossa, an issue of international importance, I lost the ladies and thus ended my quest to quench this unruly passion. The merchant opened a splendid bottle of '89 la Tour, which quenched everything else, and I bought three cases to be sent up North.

I have no hope of meeting with any woman who would please me more. Despairing of sonnets, I wrote Eliza a letter – never to be sent – confessing my regard for her. I thought it might purge out the poison. It has had the effect of pouring it directly into my veins. I wrote it, read it, slept with it under my pillow, dreamed of the scene that would result upon my proposal, awoke in a distracted fever, and burned the damned confession to an ash. All this tumult in my brain, and the innocent herself lies just two dozen miles up the Stevenage road.

24 Dec   Grosvenor Sq.

It is fixed! Dear diary do not think me a dunder-head. I have just parted with Fitzwm who has arranged for transport on an American trade ship from Brighton to Dieppe scheduled for the 27 Dec. We arrive the wake of Lord Malmsbury's departure from Paris, which apparently had little effect on the state of relations, and Pitt is resigned to unavoidable conflict. Before war is full-fledged, we shall take our leave of England for a genuine adventure. We plan to assume the identities of American brothers from the state of Virginia who speak little French and dedicate themselves to the pursuits of leisure. He has just delivered me a speech on the basic points of farming in tobacco!

Fitzwm knows not whether this alias is rendered necessary by French hostility, but cautious within our impetuousness we shall be. We plan to stay three weeks at the most – more would be risky and hard to cover. Fitzwm has also received a letter in reply from the Bayard father, renouncing his dying son and any connexion with his final days. He is a heartbroken, clearly, and having spent the better part of ten years moving past his lost son, cannot muster the will to recover back a dying expatriate into the bosom of the family. More to the point, Bayard warned Fitzwm that he will on no account take charge of his son's bastard

French offspring, who he says must be left to battle out their livelihoods among the swinish multitude. A Burkean is old Bayard, a Tory, and indeed Fitzwm believes their difference of opinion on political matters was the reason for young Bayard's ready departure for France in 1789.

Aside from curiosity, adventure, and the aid of my cousin, I have my own reasons to revisit France. I may be Darcy with old acquaintance in Paris, should they wish to see me. Justine du Pont will I hope be close by, and we may renew earlier times. We parted so strangely those seven years ago; I shall never forget her angry coldness. It initiated my fear of the power of women.

I have land lust -- for this continent or the next one over. The hedgerows and close seas scrum me in. To be American! I have scribbled a silly rhyme:

> To be brawt up on prayer-ees
> and stuffed full of crayn-berries
> to Ya-hooodle in the Appa-latch-ens
> and Ye-haw o'er the grass play-ns.
> As moun-tains rise further and further a-way,
> let's mount us a possie to search the

West way,

> where sun-down and night-time become dawn

and day.

Salty, wild America. Full of scraps of divers people and a rich terrain varied more than Britain from Greece. It is early in the America game. Fitzwm knows my mind. A parcel of a hundred thousand eastern acres on a river for ten thousand quid. A year's offerings for a fresh dimension free of all this starch. I might marry a vigorous girl and live on sun-drenched fields and work among equals. Fitzwm says Jones knows a land agent in Paris. As Bingley is to coffee and tea, am I to land. Patience.

I have sent notes to Aunt Catherine, Georgianna, the Bingleys, and a few other acquaintances to the effect of my needing immediately to proceed to Sheffield on urgent business -- something regarding a recent breakthrough in the mechanical sciences that might aid in mining operations. Gibson has agreed to answer with my humblest excuses any calls I might receive at Pemberley, and Sutton will guard over Grosvenor in the meantime. I have pre-written two bland notes to my Aunt and Georgie, to be put in the mail in a fortnight's time. How else may I escape, but by misleading everyone? The clandestine route is the only available means of liberation for the imprisoned *fils de fortune Anglais*. For the next fortnight or more, I am Caleb Williams the American, fleeing my own shadow Falkland.

1 January, 1797 Champ de Mars, Paris

Bonne Annee from the ampitheatre of the revolution! Time is not linear. I recall as yesterday the weeks in Paris nearly seven years ago when *la Constitution* was celebrated with *la Fete de la Federation*; a spectacle that still dazzles my recollection. Five hundred thousand people of all ranks singing of unity, harmony, liberty, libation; myself and Tainbridge swept up in the throngs circling in from the Tuileries and away to Notre Dame. What a blissful sendoff was Paris for my three year tour! And as the hum and nerve of the people animated the body of the city, so grew I into awareness of myself as a man; in body of course, but more in mind. A spiritual insurrection came against the old ways of England, which I myself embodied in my title, income, education, breeding, behaviour, appearance, acquisitions, and innocence. Paris and her newborn people were the playmates of my earliest adulthood. And Tainbridge! What soaked starch was the boy-man tumbling from his Cambridge tower to a Montmartre *lupanar*; what revolution of the British body and mind! I make light of his best times; old England has not dealt kindly with him since.

In the drowse of intervening years I had forgot much of that youthful *esprit de corps*. I was falling back into the old assumptions of rank, harangued by my relations and disappointed in love. Seven years has also rendered severe marks on the faces of bright Parisians. I expect to find old friends quite changed by the business of freedom and self-governance, and changed by the Terror. Mrs. Williams is still in Paris writing letters – her eighth volume came out last year in London, and it is my major source of information. London is full of desperate descriptions of the squalour, violence, and penury of France. The English imagine the Terror on every street corner, with bodies yet swinging from *les lanternes*. We have seen little of those dire reports, and I begin to find Mrs. Williams's descriptions more steady and accurate renderings of France eight years beyond the Bastille.

Fitzwm and I arrived unscathed two days ago, our packet having caught a favourable chill west wind. The captain, Whelden, allowed me to sway out the journey from the crow's nest so I could espy both countries at once for most of the journey. No sign of French stripes from the giddy mast. Fitzwm has no stomach for sea travel, but I felt nervy and wonderful, slapped by the chill salt sea air and beguiled by the mysteries that lay at our bow. Unlike Shakespeare's sea boy, I slept not. We stayed in Dieppe only so long as to steady our legs, and from thence it was two day's ride to Paris, which we took by stage. Considering the climate of warfare between our nations, and of late the rise of arms in the call for liberty, we met little to make us fearful along the public road. A few battallions were housed in Dieppe in wait for the spoils of the shipyard, a place alive with iron clangs and tar smoke. There was talk of French navy ships causing trouble for American merchants. I thought of how slender the watery margin between our nations, the trouble ahead, and I fixed my hat lower.

In public Fitzwm is Nathaniel Kirk, and I am his cousin Lindsey Kirk. We have sprung from a nurturing farm on the low hills of central Virginia, in Jefferson's region. Tobacco, horses, whiskey, and dust-kicking society are our trades -- the life I might have known had my grandparents left in the Restoration with so many other gentlemen.

We are Dixies in character, obstinate on the slave question. I recall Cowper's words: "There is no flesh in man's obdurate heart … human nature's broadest, foulest blot, chains him, and tasks him, and exacts his sweat with stripes that Mercy with a bleeding heart weeps when she sees inflicted on a beast." We expect often to be engaged with the French on questions of man's liberty, and I will play my part of the genteel Dixie, a beneficent terror to the negroes. I hope the language barrier will take the blame for my poor defenses of the tyrannical system – slaves are the blood and muscle of our colonies, but the system shall change before long. Negroes emancipated during the American Revolution are in much demand as footmen to rich families, but as footmen only have I seen them – not as labourers.

England seems a universe away across this channel. I regret her not. May old acquaintance be forgot and never brought to mind. And a Happy New Year. Tomorrow we shall call upon the long lost Henry Bayard.

2 Jan   Le Marais, Paris

We have returned from la Place Pigalle after an exhausting day. We succeeded in locating Bayard, who is desperate in his consumption, living in squalid tenement and nursed by his ancient father-in-law, who seems hardly able to empty a chamber pot, let alone care for a man who coughs dark blood and raves at the gods of cosmic injustice. The old man speaks only French but we came to understand that Bayard has lucid moments, tho' today was sadly bereft of them. Bayard did recognise Fitzwm, and cried salt tears upon his recognition of an old English friend, clasping his hand and drawing him closer only to scream oaths against King and country. I felt a kind of suffocation at the miasmic scene, and after a quarter of an hour we begged leave to take fresh air out in the street, and consult upon our plan. We gained information from the old French man that his daughter is dead of the same disease, some twelvemonth gone by, and that the boys are staying for a few days at the *petit maison* of a friend in Montmartre. This is not a permanent solution, however, and everything is in turmoil in the city – a fervid turmoil that tends towards violence at inopportune moments. We must take care to arrange for the boys, at least, and see to Bayard's funeral. We have left the *vieillard* with a few gold coins to pay for a cleaning and restocking of provisions, and promised to call again tomorrow.

I to bed.

3 Jan   Le Marais, Paris

Bayard was somewhat better today – not only did he greet us with warmth, but he was able to receive information from Fitzwm and reply in a rational manner. The place was also much improved by the kind old man, whose name is Laurent Didier, inspired as he was by gold. Both men have solemnly pledged secresy regarding our identity. They know us only as the Americans of our alias. We shared a bottle of claret with Didier in celebration of his grandsons, and also provided a robust meal the likes of which I daresay he has not ingested in years.

Fitzwm informed Bayard of his family's stalwart position regarding the boys. We had some time to generate stratagems. Didier expects not to live into the next century (and sadly I concur), so the boys (Henri is six, and Remy is three) would become orphans and left to the care of the state. That would be unacceptable in any case, but considering the disarray of government and social sectors here, it would be unthinkable. We might pay a family to bring them up properly, but that would amount to a considerable sum that neither man can afford. We might bring them back to England and hope to have them installed in Fitzwm's family, perhaps as distant cousins, to live in Yorkshire and find their way. Fitzwm is reluctant to spring upon his family a couple of frenglish whelps of uncertain health and disposition with little explanation for their appearance, and his father Devillier is not a generous-minded man; he takes after his sister Aunt Catherine more than my mother Anne. We might buy them passage to America, if only they were four or five years older. We have not hit upon the solution as yet. Fitzwm arranged for the boys to be sent to our rented rooms in La Marais for the next few weeks. My dear cousin will spoil them with *bonbons* and *jouets*.

Relaxed by the wine and good food, our conversation wandered to the present state of France. Bayard discussed Buonaparte's advances in against Austria in Italy, notably the Siege of Toulan some three years ago. More recently engineered a defeat of domestic Royalist insurrection. He is long associated with the Robespierre brothers. His name is oft mentioned in the Times as our first adversary when his attentions turn back to warfare in the north. Didier celebrates his success in northern Italy against the Austrians, though Bayard enjoined that he was set back in the battle Caldiero, and Didier replied that he found victory thereafter in Arcole. Battles fall close upon one another, and the French Republic is continually sending back to the motherland for reinforcements. Bayard lives with the fear that his sons will become boy soldiers the instant they can hold steady a musket. It seems a rational enough fear – one that we hold in England as well. We left the conversation and *la rue Pigalle* with history yet unfolding on that Southern front. After so much conversation, Bayard needed a rest.

I hear chirping voices in the parlor – the boys have arrived.

4 Jan   Le Marais, Paris

I devoted my morning to Henri and Remy, who I find to be
delightful, bright, and energetic lads. I am astonished at their
gusto. They have had a sad life, but bear none of the marks of
privation. Nor are they frivolous and silly, nor peevish and
violent-minded. With the right experience and education, they
will make admirable men, and Fitzwm and I must make an
avenue for them. We arranged for a tutor to school them for the
next fortnight, and evaluate their level of education. Remy,
barely three, is already reading and has intelligible writing!

Their cheery company gives me the heart of a father. Now I
only need a pleasing, smart girl to make me complete. I am at
liberty to chuse. All that consumed me in December seems
worlds away, except for her. She inhabits me still.

Off himself to la Place Pigalle, Fitzwm begged me to take relief
on my own today. I have had a riotous time among the lower
Parisians in the bistros. They are stuffed with pride over their
triumphs under the command of Buonaparte, known by his
Christian name Napoleon. Paris is a constant roil of high
emotion, most of it positive, but at times vicious behaviours
emerge in the street and we have heard proclamations against
England and the remaining gentle classes of France who are in
hiding in the country. Still, I believe in the original spirit of the
Revolution, now that Robespierre is put down, and I only hope
that all this talk of war is so much steam venting from an over-
fueled machine. I quaffed a fantastic vintage from Languedoc,
and toasted their sun-burnt skins.

7 Jan   Le Marais, Paris

Still I have no news of Justine, though we send out cautions queries about *la famille* DuPont and have heard some alarming accounts of their persecution during the Terror. I pray the worst has not befallen them.

Finding Jones in his office, he has introduced me to the land agent from America, Mr. Theophile Cazenove, and we have had the most enlightening conversation. He cares nothing about my Englishness, calling himself even an Anglophile and closet royalist. He also loves the wildness of his native land. We talked about the opening of the frontier to settlers, and how agriculture has extended all the way to the great continental river, the Miss-is-sippi, and joined with the French trapping settlements. That far westward is too much for my tolerance of risk, particularly as the Spanish have claims on the Western side and the Indians are by no means friendly to European settlement.

The gentleman recommended some property closer to the eastern coast, in the mountains two hundred miles distant. Both New York and Penn's woods have available plots, vast ones, under the provision of the Holland Land Company, which Cazenove represents. We discussed a piece some hundred thousand acres near the juncture of three rivers and the growing industrial city of Pittsburg. Even if I were to leave its development and occupation to a later generation, I believe it would be a good investment. The future lies in America. I have drafted a letter to Gibson and to Smithson, which Cazenove approved and I shall send it whenever I find a means of conveyance. Cazenove has promised to meet with me next week with some maps showing the available purchases. May my dreams rest there meanwhile, and away from Hertfordshire.

Jones and Cazenove have warned me of degrading relations between America and France in the wake of the States signing Jay's treaty with Britain. The treaty allies Britain with America in trade, as well as cultural sympathy. Cazenove is sanguine that the animosity will melt away to the mutual republican spirits, but Jones is convinced that the militarism of the new France, and its desperate need of revenue may make American trade ships at Calais and Dieppe a savoury mark. In short, Fitzwm and I may be *more* in danger as the Kirk brothers from Virginia than as our British selves. It depends upon on our company. We shall have to play the two roles as Kemble slides from Hardcastle to Macbeth on the London stage.

9 Jan   Le Marais, Paris

Bayard is fast growing worse, and Fitzwm and I believe he may not outlast the week. He has lapsed from lucidity into a state of desperate torpor, where his uneasy rest is broken with fits of coughing. Fitzwm has directed Didier to arrange for final rites and a funeral. We are no closer to finding a solution for his boys, who are shielded from this unpleasant business by remaining at our rooms with their tutor. I am tempted to take them on as my own wards, for who is to deny me anything? They are vigorous and worthy boys who might make merit as Englishman, and I could find a discreet place for them on my estate.

Fitzwm resists my offer, however, thus far. It stands in as a contingency plan. Then there is the snarly business of getting French boys across the channel at wartime with proper papers! Today the boys sang for me the revolutionary tune *Ça ira, ça ira*, which they would be well to seize as their anthem in coming weeks. It will come, whatever holds the future.

12 Jan   Essonne

At last I have located Justine by the wits of a post-man acquainted with her family's affairs. She is staying in Essonne outside of Paris with her brother and father. She was shocked to find a Lindsey Kirk, neé Darcy, calling at her door, and indeed my heart was in my throat and I nearly shook my boots off as I waited at the verge. She is the same as ever she was in the early parts of the Revolution – spirited, self-confident, flirtatious, and dangerous to know.

The family are ostracized and endangered in the militant climate, however, and the DuPonts plan to emigrate to America themselves, perhaps as early as this spring, to begin a gunpowder business on the east coast near the capital Philadelphia. So I have discovered Justine just in time. The family feel endangered having tried to defend the unfortunate King, and are in a state of prolonged shock over the fate of the chemist Laviosier, who lost his head to the blade some two years ago. Justine's brother, Eleuthère, continues work on improvements in explosives at the Essonne factory. Her father Pierre is acquainted with Jefferson, who plays the part of diplomat between French and American interests.

Justine and I spent our first evening in a confessional. Our relations ended abruptly at her command (see my sad outpourings in vol. 1, September 1790!), and she felt equal to explanation after this lapse of seven years. Justine has a daughter named Sabine who she claims is mine, passed off as her dead husband's. She says the realization of her condition came to her about a week after she missed her menses, only eight weeks into our acquaintance. Her instinct was to push me away and forge ahead, even if alone.

A married French woman and an English youth *en tour* on the eve of certain international conflict – it was too dangerous to continue – at least that is her defence. She gave me no explanation of her coldness at the time, and it utterly devastated me, uninitiated in matters of the heart as then I was. Knowing now the circumstances, I must forgive her. I only briefly saw the girl on her way to school today, and I know not what to think. Fortunately Justine expects no money, no alliance, no mentorship between me and Sabine. Justine of course never expected to see me again, especially after the war broke out. She says she simply *tenait a te dire*.

It is better for the girl to appear as a legitimate child of a tragically dead father, and the family has easily enough resources to support Sabine through a good education. Her uncle the chemist is already tutoring her on theories of matter and advances in electricity, and allows her to linger in his laboratory *chez soi*. Sabine reminds me keenly of Georgie as a young girl – slight, graceful, shy, deferent, and lovely. She is more like her aunt than like her mother.

I am not horrified by the idea of having a *le fruit de la passion* breathing in the world, especially if she is well cared for, educated, and has a future in America. The DuPonts are Huguenots at least. I feel lucky to have been instructed in the *art de l'amour* by an older woman who holds no remorse or expectations about our future together. Justine has always been her own woman, with an independent mind often indifferent to male company. Her energy and independence were the headwaters of my admiration. I could, of course, throw everything over and follow the DuPonts to America as I might have done seven years ago. But that time of happy madness is past. I must attend to my future when I return to England.

Justine's husband was killed in the Terror, as old Lebrun was the very embodiment of bleary-eyed *vie de luxe* that the lower orders so hated (his sacrifice was *un cadeau de Dieu à la main de la Revolution*, she jests). She was spared by her wits and connexions among the revolutionaries, and her father Pierre was even luckier. He was condemned to death, but spared that fate by the timely sacking of Robespierre. In spite of all this harassment, the DuPonts remain supportive of the revolutionary cause and the new Federation, tho' not its desperate means.

How wild to revisit old haunts and past selves and find everything uncanny – familiar but oh the difference! I am released from the torment of loving Justine in vain, and I feel in utter command of myself in her presence. These intervening years have left their mark, however, as I vowed never again to be overwhelmed with hopeless affection, but always to hold command over my emotions and my expressions of regard. Justine's cold dismissal made a frozen man of me. Now I hope to thaw again. *Tout comprendre c'est tout pardonner*.

We were left reminiscing about the joie de vie of 1790, when I was an innocent boy of privilege, lately orphaned, and she an unhappily married and free-thinking woman. Until the moment of seeing her again, I had forgot how enamoured I was with her independence and confidence. I was quite in love. She taught me much how to be embodied and passionate, how to treat a woman. Then she ended it in a rage – a few fortnights of fabulous madness and a long wintery aftermath. At last I have an answer, in the form of a healthy child – wondrous kind! So long I have slept and forgotten about women ever since – asleep in ball rooms, asleep at card tables, asleep over insipid conversations about finery and ladies' accomplishments. If only the English woman were allowed to be worldly, independent, a bit more French!

Though Justine looks seven years older she is still quite vigorous. She is hale, sharp, and alluringly *supérieure*. After a bottle of Burgundy, she proposed revisiting our *petit amour*, should I wish it, for our mutual pleasure. Not with an idea of a lasting attachment. Being unattached and with pointed desire, I shall again take comfort here. I trust myself, and feel not in danger with her. Tho' she may mean to manipulate me again, I am in command of myself. There is something of EB in Justine – not in appearance, but in spirit. Is it wrong to pretend?

13 Jan   Essonne

Today Justine took me to see her brilliant young brother, Eleuthère, at the gunpowder works in Essonne. The lad is a few years younger than myself, and was only a stripling in 1790. He was tutored by Lavoisier in chemistry and wields his education with great energy. Sabine's uncle has his little pupil piping off the latest advances in chemical theory and the conservation of mass. Eleuthère is cheeky -- he could not refrain from teasing me about Britain's loss of the colonies in America, and celebrate France's parallel revolutionary history that promises to make the two new nations great allies. *Votre Roi est fou, et il a perdu le plus beau paradis du monde en même temps que sa tête.* Having heard my own father express similar sentiments twenty years ago when I was a boy, I could not disagree with him. The American colonies were our greatest loss of the eighteenth century. I only observed that King George lost his head in a more favourable way, the metaphorical, than much of the French nobility. We were in complete agreement.

Eleuthère is an optimistic man, able to set aside the Terrors of recent years and look to a happy future in that land of possibilities. The family plans to purchase lands in the American state named after Baron De-la-warr, just down the river of the same name about twenty miles from the national capital in Philadelphia. The whole family is full of utopian spirit about founding a new life in America free from the bondage of monarchy, in a land stuffed with raw materials to work into goods, and game to hunt on unfettered land. With their intelligence and energy I can only suppose they will find success. Justine's brother is also a passionate naturalist who wishes for wider ranges to explore, though I expect his new

American business will keep him at factory. When I think of my lands in Derbyshire, of their groomed woods, fenced farms, and enclosed wastes, the wilderness of America sets my heart racing again. Like two women of my imagination, one of discernment and breeding, one of passion and spontaneity, I love them both.

The DuPonts are extremely well connected. The father Pierre is a close political ally of Jefferson. Eleuthère hinted that the present territory of America will soon be vastly extended westwards of the Mississippi river to include land currently controlled by France and Spain. I only imagine the Indians will defend their claim as well.

January 14   Essonne, Paris

Justine's *etudes des arts de l'amour* have recommenced. I am too torn with desire to resist her. I may ease my passions for another through this *catharsis*, and Justine has always been open to *dalliance*. She treats me still as an innocent, a pupil in the fleshly arts. Little has changed in the lapse of time but for the all-important revolution in my self-knowledge.

I understand Justine better now that I have years of perspective behind me. However engaging her manner, her heart is not easily touched. An ardent lover, she is easily cast in a state of infatuation that makes her mad with pledges, poetry, and pathos. She is intelligent and comely, and makes a man believe he is the only creature to roam the earth on two legs. But she is also a creature of whim whose love is a form of self-flattery, and her opinions of herself are as capricious as her feelings about others. She is happiest when insane with a particular passion, but before long, as quickly as she falls in love, her passion dries in the hot siroccos of change that oft befall the young. She becomes depressed and thinks less of herself, and therefore less of the object that so filled her with the happy delusion of love. *Joie de vie* sinks into *ennui*. And thereafter, another turn of the cycle.

She keeps her emotional distance by adopting the role of instructress, rather than equal in passion. It is a form of play-acting: the school-mistress and the pupil. She says she wishes to prepare me for my *marie Anglaise*, and in her opinion English men know not the first stroke when it comes to pleasing women in the arts of love. We are not deficient in mind or body, but in the soul and sentiment of the act, and its choreography. Justine's *école* operates on four principales: First, *toujours, toujours plus lentement*, second, *maintenir du contact avec ses yeux*, and third, *le corps de la femme est plus sensitive que cela de l'homme – tout de sa corps est un organe sexuel*. Always go more slowly. Keep contact with her eyes – the windows of the soul. A woman's whole body is a sexual organ – treat it with like respect, and neglect none of its potential. Finally, *votre plaisir passe apres tout le reste – le plus grand plaisir est celui qui se fait attendre* – my pleasure comes last – the longest awaited pleasure is the best. I believe I have acquitted myself rather well with these *quatre principe de l'amour*. Justine was speechless after my full recitation.

So I have just emerged from a whole day in bed to claim my own separateness and to catch a wink of sleep. My concern is not that I shall not know what to do with my virgin English wife, but that I find a wife who fully excites my desire to recite *les quatre principe*, and perhaps invent a few more. As I was in this compromising position, bare-skinned and bearing my soul, I confessed to Justine my hopeless love for an English country girl. I described her ineffable charms. It was even more pleasant to talk of love, than to act on the physical impulse. Justine heard me with sympathy. She believes that the body chuses the mate, not the mind, and she sees that my inability to fully understand or rationalize my passion for EB is its most promising stamp of genuineness. It is, she says, *le vrai chose*. She advised me to stay wise to desire lest I lose all memory of the miracle of an embodied life. *La fortune n'est pas l'or, c'est l'amour.*

It is wonderful to possess myself again – to be recovered from the tumult of having been cast away, unloved, as a pebble thrown back to the waves. Understanding each other, Justine and I may be friends again. And I may again trust in love.

With Justine's help, I have a notion about the future fortune of the Bayard boys in America. Fitzwm writes to hasten my return to Paris, to see out the last hours of Henry Bayard.

18 Jan   Le Marais, Paris

Two days ago I rejoined Fitzwm in Paris, having torn myself away from the DuPonts.

I shared with Fitzwm my idea for Henri and Remy to accompany the DuPonts to America as cousins of the family, and to share in that future whatever it may provide. He was elated with the notion, and amazed at the generosity of a family who would adopt two young boys with hardly another thought. Yea, though they may be working at chemical equations in a murky factory through their whole youth! They are more likely to have the joy of true freedom in a new home.

In my absence from our apartment at Le Marais, Cazenove delivered a fair map of three plots of land I might purchase for ten thousand. I spent the morning combing over their descriptions, and settled upon one. I delivered this news to him in person along with a cheque down-payment of ten percent, and he sent word back to his office in Philadelphia to withhold any other purchase of it. It lies upon the river Monongahela, full west in the state of Pennsylvania, among the low and wooded Appalachian mountains. Ten miles of it front upon the river, which Cazenove describes as somewhat shallow and not yet navigable by trade ships, but sweet in water. The plot lies south of the city of Pittsburgh, and he assures me that within twenty years a series of locks will be installed to make it a trade route to

Virginia. Two other rivers – the Allegheny and Ohio, join in Pittsburgh, and I might purchase land upon them, but Cazenove has advised me to chuse the southwards plot because of the lower prices and greater wilderness. As I am indeed somewhat at his mercy, I have agreed upon more land (over one hundred thousand acres – one hundred fifty square miles) for the reduced price of nine thousand pounds.

I received the gratifying counsel and support of Pierre DuPont, who was that afternoon in town. His research into American land has been thorough, and the price per acre cannot be gainsaid, though its remoteness is an obstacle. DuPont has chosen land at a much higher price within the fall line near the coast and the capital at Philadelphia so as to facilitate trade, but I have no such ambitions. I shall call my land Monon for the time being, in honour of its river. We have exchanged the necessary documents and I shall close the business with Smithson upon returning to England.

20 Jan   La Place Pigalle

May Bayard rest in peace. Surrounded by his care-taker Didier, Fitzwm and myself, Henri and Remy, a clergyman, and a few sympathetic neighbors, Bayard bid adieu to this world quietly. His bright eyes and gleaming face, wasted and made weird by consumption, looked forth to the next world with patience and forbearance. There was no raving in the end.

Adding to his peace, Fitzwm murmured in his ear the news of the *famille* DuPont offer for his sons, and his faint smile and nod was a full acquiescence to the plan.

We have made arrangements for his burial at the Protestant cemetery, and the ceremony will take place tomorrow. Once the boys have been looked over by a doctor for any signs of their father's illness, we will all proceed out to Essonne at our earliest convenience. We shall not delay any longer than necessary – I hope to travel out tomorrow after the funeral. Fitzwm is in a state of transport over this good fortune – the DuPonts are wealthy, intelligent, kind, and have great prospects in that land of infinite possibility. We plan to break the news of their adoptive family to the boys tomorrow, after their father is interred.

22 Jan   Essonne

We are all snug in the DuPont *maison* – the three children Sabine, Henri, Remy being newly acquainted and already thick in friendship and sympathy. Justine is thrilled to have two *frères de coeur* for her daughter, and Sabine looks to make an excellent elder sister to them both. The doctor delivered a clean bill of health – *Merci de Dieu* – and the male DuPonts are pleased to extend their family outwards in these difficult times. The boys are overwhelmed – with the death of their father, their mother before them, and this new whirl of circumstance centered on the new country across the sea! The three chicks retired to their chamber with the nurse just after dinner, and tomorrow they will wake as siblings.

26 Jan   La Campagne

I have for every year since my acquaintance with Justine kept up an experiment of the brain's imagination, by taking a dose of laudanum. My agreement with myself is that I will take the anodyne no more than twice per year, at a time of my choosing. Fitzwm is keen to try for the first time, tired as he is of the last month of exertion and grief, and I have agreed to be his escort through the opiate depths. We are to be Homer's Lotos-Eaters, content to dwell in a lovely limbo far from the tyranny of reason, monarch, property, and society. Justine has arranged for the children at Essonne, and will meet us this evening here with her *chère amie*, Julie Lamont.

Before leaving our post in La Marais, I received word from Gibson that all is quiet in Pemberley and London is a snooze, and he sent my pre-written letters ahead to Georgie, Bingley, and my Aunt, who thank God is returned to Rosings. When spring comes she will re-hatch her pecking brood of demands.

How do the ladies of Hertfordshire spend their time? By now EB may have accepted her cousin so as to protect Longbourn. It makes me shiver. I push the image away as too awful, perverse, disgusting, wasteful. His fat fingers upon her breasts, his scratching whiskers at her neck. I must inquire as to her fate upon return to London. With such images already in my mind, dare I trust the opium to drive them further towards vivid expression?

28 Jan   Le Campagne

In the last two days we have passed an eternity. Our party – Fitzwm, Justine, Julie, and myself, passed around the laudanum, fifteen drops each dissolved in a small glass of cognac. It is not really a social drug – opium tends to drive one deeper into one's own predilections and make the sober world and other people appear bizarre, perverse, unreachable, like one is sinking from the surface of a lake filled with pleasure boats down, down, seeing only the shadowy hulls above, hearing sounds warped and tortured, and finding kinship with scuttling crabs and flashing fish. That is a sketch of my first experience years ago. I shall now describe yesterday's:

Throughout the whole I was haunted by Blake's proverbs of Hell, and the chains of indoctrination he bemoans. We were in as pleasant a place as France can offer these days – a quiet farm with a warm wood fire in the house and plenty of roaming space beyond its doors. Thus, I lived in two worlds, the inner world of devils, a hot place where Justine and Julie caressed by the fire and murmured their perceptions in inscrutable French, and a cold, outer place where Fitzwm was striding over the fallow fields, ranting and crying and laughing and bargaining to a ghostly angelic presence.

Blake's poem reverses the value of these two spaces, imaging hell and devils as lusty, almost virtuous creatures, and angels as prim, terrorizing, hypocritical monsters. Through the window I perceived that Fitzwm was battling in the cold field with a tyrannical angel that had formed from the vapours of his own breath, and I felt a burst of nerve and energy course through me as he swung through the air at the phantom, then fell to his knees laughing. It was not him, exactly, not my cousin, but some embodiment of English valour who triumphed before me. It sounds ridiculous, and mad, I'm well aware, but it was as weighty an impression as a brain can forge.

I felt unequal to the heat and closeness of the indoors, so I ranged abroad, perceiving every sound of nature as a kind of improvisational symphony – animals bleating, birds scuffling in fallen leaves, a surprised fox barking at me twice, then settling into a deep gaze over my soul, before dashing off into eternity. The fox had Elizabeth's eyes – bright and perceptive, infinite in depth, windows into the abyss. Though I entreated her to return I never saw it again. Each one of these animal encounters was bracingly intimate, sublime, spiritual, sensual. The trees were gigantic gentle friends, enormous, stout fungi, and I clasped their trunks and rubbed my half-bearded face against their kind roughness. It felt as though every nerve ending in my body was a set of eyes, ears, and lips, and I could perceive everything with magnified senses – I might leap up to the heavens and perceive the heavy old globe turning beneath me. Each minute (strange tyrannical measure!) was an eon. I climbed a tree with tears streaming down my face, limb by limb a staircase to the sky, and the ground grew small. Fitzwm in the field was a little brown atom feathered in the infinite atmosphere.

I scribbled some of my opiate impressions on scrap paper at the moment of returning to the farm house. Here I record them, disparate and boggled as they are:

Infinity explodes every moment to the open mind.

I would hawk Pemberley at the circus fair for a free life with EB.

Future is west. Past is east. Present is this ink's outline, senseless without the mind.

I triumph over the abyss by letting go of the cliff.

I am nothing more than a latter-day mollusc.

Fitzwm is insane with joy; he grabbles like an idiot boy.

We have lost *les soeurs* J & J in the sweet light of *fait de l'amour*. They love each other.

Time and space are self-same only spread across four dimensions.

My greatest humanity is unquenchable lust. Long live my thirst!

I am an automaton and a villain when I follow *les regles de l'ancien regime*.

Best to be an impoverished dunce with bright dreams.

Custom is my gaol, and I spy a loose bar in its window.

Darcy is a pinto running free on western plains.

Darcy is an eagle, peering from the sky at the mousy little men.

I am a grand old oak, rooted in the river bank with branches growing to heaven and leafed in winter with the stars. The oaks are swarms of atoms.

I shall live 30,000 days. Today is my 10,731st. How shall a free man spend his wealth?

From the blistered mountain top, I am a cataract crashing to the fertile valley.

Lindsey Kirk of Virginia dreams of white skin under horsewhips.

The sun forsakes us, as does the poppy muse.

These were my written thoughts. After completing this wild trip into the world of the opiate imagination, we fell into restless sleeps in heaps on the floor – I imagine it was quite a dissolute scene of the opium den, if seen by sober eyes.

I was harangued by horrid dreams where my wishes to be close to EB were realised (happy moment! I kissed her naked hand), only to have her melt away into the sneer of Aunt Catherine delivering unto me a disorderly, shivering Anne, festering with wounds inflicted by a French mob. I snatched up Anne and was running through narrow streets in a labyrinth where each new turn was an uncanny repetition of what had come before, when at last I came to an open door and pushed my way through. It was a close, dark room and I put down my fainting burden, quite unresponsive, and looked around me, when suddenly Mrs. Bennet emerged from the shadows and threw a lever on the wall and underneath me the floor fell and I surrendered to gravity and infinite darkness, yelling as I woke myself from this hell-scape of my own creation.

My head aches, and we have agreed to cook a simple meal and attempt sleep again until we naturally wake. Teazed and tormented again in dreams, I terribly miss the bright presence of that intimate stranger. Would that she had been here in body, as she seemed present to my spirit! My companions are good people whom I admire and love, but friends cannot always stand in for passions. Striving to recover from this infatuation has only deepened it. Tonight, those feelings feel fortunate, like they are a wealth entirely beyond ten thousand a year. Who is this great illustrious lord the world takes me for? I am a poor fool with a lover's dazzled smile.

29 Jan   La Campagne

Fitzwm and I spent the morning discussing our impressions of yesterday. He thinks he defeated the whole French army, embodied in General Napoleon, on the frozen field of battle. He is both stimulated and unnerved by the vivid impression of this phantom fight. What can the mind be, that it is so transformed by a few dusky drops of the poppy? We wondered over the chemical nature of perception, and whether God is in the poppy, or we are merely an emergent conglomerate of chemical impressions, thrown this way and that by tobacco, liquor, laudanum, love, and lust. Fitzwm is more devout that I, but we agreed that religion holds not the final answer. It is only one chain of stories among many. Is there a science of the brain?

Today we bid goodbye to Justine and Julie. I am content to find Justine well-pleased with a new *petite amie*, and I am not scandalized by the intimacy between women. Who am I to disapprove of ardent feelings? Our different dispositions – hers vigorous, open, and capricious, mine cautious, reserved, and steady – split a rift between us those years ago, and that chasm echoes now again. I am no longer in love with Justine, but I do find her to be one model of a modern woman – self-confident with a true superiority of mind, liberated, educated, and independent. But Justine is not for me, and I am not for her. It is refreshing to be frank with a woman who is an intimate, but not be so infatuated as to become a spoony. She gave me hope that my madness for EB is the sweetest form of reason. The modern marriage rewards genuine inclination and casts sand in the eye of avarice.

Justine assures me she will keep me apprised of the DuPont fortunes when they reach America, and should I ever find myself upon those shores I will contact them. I also begged further news of Sabine and her new brothers. Julie is to go to America as well, and Justine has pledged never to marry again. Fitzwm and I left them after *pain et café* in the morning, to live out their private day. They return to the family in Essonne tomorrow.

There is nothing else to say. *Bon voyage, bonne chance, adieu.*

31 Jan   Le Marais, Paris

Winter sets in deeper in Paris, and the charade grows tiresome. I begin to feel home-sick, and the climate in France is degrading against both British and Americans. I am sure Georgie misses me, and I have become neglectful to my duties at home. It has been exactly a month, and even the slow nature of correspondence cannot explain my absence. We have begun to inquire about a return passage.

1 February   Le Marais, Paris

We spent much of the evening at *Le Taureau*, an everyman's watering hole, swilling ale amidst reeking pipes of tobacco, and something sweet smelling they call *chanvre*, meting out my French with what semblance of an ambiguous accent I can garner. Fitzwm is much more liquid in tongue than I. As the danger is not absent in this spy-riddled quarter, I find my natural laconic state convenient for once. We believe that these lower orders of French are still positively disposed towards America, whatever their diplomats may do to insult American emissaries. The underclasses of France imagine the British, not the

Americans, to be their boogey-men, since we still genuflect to George upon his throne.

An old lady Mme. Canard engaged me in conversation in which she reminisced about the executions at *La Place de la Revolution* during the Terror. It seems she was a voracious *Tricoleuse*, smearing the spatterings of the spectacle on her upturned lips and returning the next day for more fare. She leaned to my ear and whispered, *Le sang goute comme le sperme*, and dissolved in a pile of cackles from which I despaired to escape. *Mais c'est plus nourissant!* she amused. However, in a moment she turned deadly serious and grabbed my arm, leaning again into my ear she carefully pronounced, *Le roi d'Angleterre reigne dans l'enfer*. I kept my countenance and feigned not to comprehend. Seeing me not moved towards joy as she supposed an American might be at such a sentiment, she turned to the general rabble and repeated *Le roi d'Angleterre! Reigne dans l'enfer!* each cadence striking her fist on the board and her goblet a swinging pendulum in the air. Fitzwm turned a furtive eye my way and surrounding revelers picked up the couplet in unison, each swinging his glass and striking his fist to the rhythm, *Le roi d'Angleterre! Reigne dans l'enfer!* The sheer joy on their flushed faces as their imaginations painted King George inferno I shall never forget, lit as it was by ale and smoke and the great fireplace of the public house.

The war is coming with greater fury. They kept up *en chantant* for many minutes, Fitzwm and I feigning to enjoy the moment where the freedom of Americans from English taxes was chanted as vile analogy for Robespierre's triumph over Marie Antoinette. As they settled back to wetting their throats, Fitzwm somewhat weakly ejaculated *Washington bras, Adams cerveau, Jefferson coeur – vive les États-Unis!* We left the place with all subtle haste, the crowd picked up *Vive la Revolution! L'enfer pour grands segnieurs!* pounding out the words as they recalled their old kingdom on its knees with its dusted coiffure over a basket. I had not the chance to bid Mme. Canard *bonne nuit* – and Fitzwm and I agree we must return to the land of the hell king before the war – with England and America -- makes travel impossible.

5 Feb   The Moon Swell Inn, Brighton

We were fortunate to find return passage on an American packet smuggling French cognac from Dieppe to a sandy landing at Beachy Head. Favourable winds ushered us, and we avoided notice from the French navy, thank God. The skipper, Weston, an American from the port of Savannah, was thankful for any gold that fell his way to aid stocking for the passage from England back to America. We are safe in Albion – unpacked with casks of cognac!

Smelling luscious of spirits, exhausted and renewed in love of country, we had a fine passage. It was all the more memorable as Fitzwm and I assisted the Americans in the hasty unpacking of their contraband from the ship to the landing boat, which was then hauled up the beach to higher ground by waiting assistants, muscular British blokes who were paid with swigs and vittles. Their ringleader paid solid gold for the load of spirits, and Weston broke open a large wheel of brie, sausages, and baguette on the beach. We made a feast like Saxon savages on this Norman finery. Weston then forged ahead in his ship to a legitimate landing at Brighton, where he means to offload the remainder of his cotton and acquire a load of woolen textiles and weapons to sell in America. American cotton becomes French cognac becomes British wool and weapons, and around the cycle turns. Weston refuses to land on the Slave Coast, at least not the African one.

We broke away from the jolly gang of thieves, a bit tipsy from joy and vertigo, and caught a late mail coach to Brighton. We will finish our journey to London in the morning, where I will visit the Bingleys and close the American land deal with Smithson. By next week I hope to return to Pemberley.

7 Feb   Grosvenor Square

I am astonished and pleased by how little happened in my absence. Sutton has kept my town house free of inquisitions on my whereabouts, by pleading that it is beneath his station as gentleman's butler to bother himself with the details of a rough trade town like Sheffield, or to report his master's business to every curious caller. Sutton is a great man for striking down gossip and nonsense dead in its track – his spine stacks tall and his lips curl to prim defiance whenever propriety is in question.

The Times' greatest news of England is that the Prince of Wales and his lackeys dined with the East India Directors at the London Tavern; and that the infant Princess Charlotte has a fever, but she is attended each breath by Dr. Warren. The trifling nature of this national news, set in contrast to the war reports from Mantua and the outrage in Dublin that points towards absolute revolution at the cries of Wolfe Tone, rejoin my happy sense that England is a space of relative tranquility dearly bought by our military endeavours and our watery moat, which keep us safe from tumult in *Europa*.

I have one small matter of business to attend to – a missive from Gibson regarding vagrants in Pemberley woods. Mrs. Reynolds espied smoke emerging from the trees on the northern slopes, and had Sinclair and his sons investigate. With Mooredun, the bailiff, Sinclair discovered three absconded soldiers, dressed in shreds and covered in horse blankets stolen from my stables, huddled by their small fire. They put up no resistance, threatened no violence, and haunted Sinclair with tales of their voyages to the torrid zone. It seems I might prosecute them for the trespass, the blankets, the inconvenience, whatever I wish. As Lord of the manor the law serves me. But as they are former soldiers returned from the West Indies with no means to support them, I cannot morally take such a severe course. I have sent word to Gibson to try and find work for them at Pemberley or in Lambton. Also I sent ahead a packet with a letter, a new gown, and bonnet for Georgianna's pleasure selected from among some exquisite India muslins in Bond street.

After the laudanum adventure, I spent the afternoon looking through this strange poem, *The Marriage of Heaven and Hell* – which is seeded with the most bizarre and brazen ideas about the villainy of the Church of England. It is fresh and subversive stuff. My favourite portion is the proverbs of Hell. I am no literary scholar, so will not occupy these pages with interpretation, but his images remain inked in my mind. He wishes to cleanse the doors of perception by sloughing off convention – class, church, monarchal government – and then he proposes we might see some infinity beyond.

He has one line that particularly struck me:

How do you know but every bird that cuts the airy way is an immense world of delight

closed by your senses five?

Is the man mad with opium, as I was in France? That is the nearest to his visions that I can identify, but I cannot simply dismiss it as mad ranting. It is entirely innovative, and notably strange. Blake argues for an ineffable infinity beyond the sensuous realm -- no bland inaccessible noumenal notion such as the Ancients and Kant would propose, but instead an exquisite material realm from which we are closed by our dull quotidian consciousness. Blake urges us to scrub it off – all our assumptions and dread perceptions, and open the doors of our sixth and seventh senses. Is it a form of intuition – like the sublime, which causes splendid horror though without an apparent cause? Is my hopeless regard for EB a symptom of greater, mysterious powers of attraction opening to something new – the bird that is an immense world of delight? Blake shows how our expectations of the roles we ought to fill in society are really just blinders at the service of our corrupt institutions. Any observer of King George cannot fail to see the aptness of his claims. It is weird and wondrous.

I will visit Johnson tomorrow to inquire after the purchase of this volume, and call on the Bingleys.

8 Feb   Grosvenor Square

I have sent off the dandy footman, Bloom, to Hertfordshire to do some sleuthing for me. He is a discreet and clever fellow, and served as my valet whilst I was at Netherfield, so he knows the faces of the persons of interest. I wish to attain intelligence as to the status of the Bennets. He will return within three days, and then I really must hasten north to see Georgianna.

I filled my day with a visit to Bingley, and also called on Johnson in his shop at St. Paul's. Bingley is entirely consumed in the new arrangements to expand their family trade domestically – to Liverpool and Manchester, and internationally – shifting sources from coffee in the West Indies towards tea in Bengal and points eastwards. Bingley's current mission is to research coffee plantations that might be established in East Africa. I have never seen the jolly dear fellow so seriously dedicated to intellectual pursuits. He was layered in maps of obscure jungles, making notes of wooly rivers and hostile tribes. The truth is, between the Great Pyramids and the Cape of Good Hope, very little is known beyond the coastlines. Only a few white explorers, mostly Portuguese and Dutch, have ventured upriver more than a few miles. Bingley is convinced that South Africa and the eastern coast south of Abyssinia will become vital colonies in our new century. He joked that he is the explorer

Mungo Park's shadow double, seeking and striving in the jungle of books and tallies of his cold dark London rooms. Bingley seemed thin and rattled in body and spirit. His studies in trade so occupying his mind, I fortunately was required to report but little of the previous month of my life.

Bingley's three youngest sisters, not yet out in society, ages 14, 12, and 9, crept into the African studies room whilst we were talking, and joined into our researches of the great Atlas. They love to pronounce the exotic names – Zanzibar, Mozambique, Zambesi – and trace the wandering lines of the East coast and the inward mountain range but little known in Abyssinia. Lucy, the youngest, pronounced with her little nose held high that she intends to marry a missionary and be among the first to hunt the beasts and make Christian the people, in service of God and country. Said Charles, You should have to become more serious and devout, Lucy, to catch a gentleman of such sober persuasion and convert the wild tribes of Africa to our staid English ways. Oh! Then, she said, I shall dress in knickers and sneak aboard a whaler in Liverpool so I may sail 'round the Cape of Good Hope seeking the great Leviathans! I defy you to stop me, Charlie. Her brother, smiling, said he would spy her on the moon by the turn of the century, if he could persuade Herschel to look through his great telescope. Then she might wed with the nebulae. Lucy has pluck and independence absent in her eldest sisters. I soon left the Bingleys to their studious teazing.

Thereafter I went to Johnson, ever in his shop, and he has invited me to a large dinner Sunday night with the leading radical intellects in his circle. I could not resist such an opening – what welcome change to spend an evening in the company of innovators rather than the fat old complaisants in society saloons. And yet I am the very figure of the man they think they detest!

Johnson declined to sell me any volume of Blake, as copies of the illuminated texts are severely limited – the poet produces them himself, in his workshop of copper plates and acids, and his wife paints them, each one different from the others. I returned my loan, and suggested that paper reprints with only the text be circulated. He assuaged me by producing a volume of Blake's *Poetical Sketches*, from 1783, which he says cry out against King George's treatment of the American colonies. Johnson is concerned that he is soon to be prosecuted for sedition for his relationship with Thomas Paine's writing.

Foul, London weather kept me indoors after dark, within my library. I receive no callers, and have instructed Sutton to tell everyone I am at my club. When they find me not at my club, the mazy streets of London must then be supposed my wandering place.

10 Feb   The Blue Boar Tavern, High Holborn

I've been at Smithson's office at Gray's Inn to discuss my recent acquisition in America. Though Smithson shrinks from any expenditure beyond bread and a roof, he does not deny that I am master of my own expenditures, and his office is merely to minimize the damage of extravagance. I handed over the bill of sale and title, which he found to be legitimate, and we have scheduled a regular payment of the balance at one thousand one hundred per annum, to be finished in eight years. He suggests that I indulge my curiosity in my investment by hiring a man from Jones's office in Philadelphia to travel to the landholding out West and prepare a detailed report of its terrain, timber, aspect on the river, and any other points of interest. I met the prospect with delight.

Smithson will write without delay, requesting that the hired man be someone who is trained in the art of surveying, natural history, and who also has an artist's hand able to draw up some fair sketches of the landscape. Such divers work may require multiple men. I am prepared to part with another two hundred to see the work done. I hope to have the report in hand by the end of the year 1797. Who knows when I may ever see the place in person?

We raised a pint of India ale to the proposition, and I secretly celebrated breaking Smithson out of his office before midnight. But alas! He is now gone back again.

12 Feb   Grosvenor Square

I am just returned from a long exhilarating Sunday dinner at Johnson's, who fills his table with such opinionated personages as makes my head spin, so stark is the contrast from the settled conservatism of the gentry. It was wonderful. Most notable was a Dr. Erasmus Darwin, who shared his opinions on natural parturition, dry-tongue fevers, chronic rheumatism, and his various notions on the evolution of forms from lower to higher orders, which he extends from the French naturalists. He has put the ideas to verse, tetrameter quatrains, and directed my attention to the loves of the plants in pollen and nectar! I caught Johnson's wink across the table, as Johnson writes severe and pointed reviews of even his favourite authors.

Dr. Darwin also recommends small doses of opium for myriad complaints, and we had a long exchange on the effects to the mind and imagination rendered by an anodyne of laudanum. Though not entirely approving of using opium for what he called "diversion," he was in support of measured experimentation to discern the effects of chemicals on the organ of thought, which remains a complete mystery to men of science. Other respected men, the chemist Humphrey Davy, and the economist Thomas Malthus, also attended. The latter is soon to publish an essay on population, in which he argues against the perfectibility of man by the principles of Enlightenment. Would that Godwin had been there, as Johnson says he often is. There would be a noggin-butting worthy of this dazzling age of science and philosophy!

The artists were represented by the Swiss painter Fuseli, master of the supernatural sublime, and the lady poet Mrs. Barbauld, a noted abolitionist and lamentress of our national sins. We circled the universe of ideas in the course of four hours, and I left un-tarred and un-feathered despite being an idle gentleman. I gained their respect by revealing some of my first-hand accounts of contemporary Paris.

Now if only I had an intimate with whom to discuss these new ideas. A lonely good-night.

13 Feb   Grosvenor Square

Bloom has returned from Hertfordshire with wondrous news. My soul softens. The villagers say that no young lady has recently wed but one – the former Miss Lucas, who I met at several gatherings, has surrendered herself to Mr. Collins – the Bennet cousin and heir to Longbourn, the bilious toady. Ah yes, I see in my entry of 27 Nov I thought him a "blowsy, foolish bloke" and an "obsequious milksop." Just so. A smirking, serpentine sycophant. If I understood their relations correctly at the Netherfield ball, there can be no other answer but that Eliza rejected a proposal from him. She is still free. She has not given herself to a fathead merely to assure a comfortable living.

Brave girl!

But there is more. The sly Bloom, in the appearance of a new recruit to the militia, fell into conversation with the gossiping Mrs. Phillips, who informed him that her niece, the eldest but one, is planning to visit her newly wed friend at Hunsford on Rosings Park during the Easter season. Mrs. Phillips sneered at the idea of her niece visiting a friend who is to become mistress at Longbourn upon the death of Mr. Bennet. Still, she is curious of their domestic arrangements, and only feared that her niece was not so good a gossip as her younger sisters and might not come out with all the lurid details of the Collins benefactress. Bloom also extracted the news that Wickham is engaged to another young woman, a Miss King, who has inherited some modest fortune. May Miss King be looked after by her relations, and kept in the warm side of fortune.

Bloom set eyes on EB herself as she accompanied her youngest sisters into town, and overheard their enthusiasm for all the new bonnets in a shop window. He distinctly heard the youngest Bennet intone, "let's buy this horrid one for Mary and see if her face by comparison renders it pretty!" How could that rational bright girl emerge from a climate of such inveterate nastiness? Yet the younger Miss Bennets behave not so differently in discourse from Caroline and Louisa, whose wealth alone brings them respect.

Well, to continue. Bloom was contemplating a window of new gentleman's hats and haberdashery next door, and before he had the chance to move on before the ladies overtook him, he found Lydia herself addressing him, though a total stranger, in the midst of the street! "La, sir. You are a supple gallant to favour our main street. Are you not wild to make love to Meryton's young ladies? May I present myself as Lydia Bennet, a ripe and eager maiden." Bloom blustered after an answer, but Elizabeth actually grabbed Lydia's collar and directed her to pass further down the street. Bloom had only to step aside for this sad parade. He thought Elizabeth might have flashed recognition, though his hair was carefully oiled and combed back in a fashion unlike he had worn it at Netherfield last fall. She said nothing, however, attending as she was to the concealment of her sister's self-exposures.

I am transported, giddy, to hear that she is out of danger from the proposals of two dastardly rivals. How perverse that I should identify Collins and Wickham as my equals! It shows the level of my infatuation with that sublime lovely creature. I miss her.

I shall invite myself to Rosings to see the apple blossoms. May my own charms pollinate the local flowers! I am resolved to finish this infatuation, either by claiming her as mine, or finding the faults to ruin her in my regard. I shall kiss, or dismiss.

14 Feb   Grosvenor Sq.

A package is dispatched with a letter to my Aunt requesting her hospitality at Eastertide. It is made weighty with the merit of a new seven-volume history of Kent that dedicates a full three pages to the architecture and ownership of Rosings Park. I have sent sugary compliments to my cousin Anne accompanied by a parcel of Dr. James's analeptic pills, which promise the health and longevity of an Eastern Buddou, however fatigued, sedentary, or gouty the constitution. Perhaps Anne will improve, not by her mother's scolding, but by rather believing herself to feel improved by the medical arts. A sugar pill may do as much, or more good, than our cleverest of poisonous concoctions. I trust James's herbal genius is at least as salubrious as sugar.

All this bosh to say that I have contrived a reunion with Elizabeth Bennet – my sole romantic mission fixed upon this St. Valentine's day. May Chaucer and the courtiers salute me.

16 Feb   Pemberley

I have made the entire journey in two days, averaging nearly eight miles per hour post-chaise. Sutton will follow within a few days, once Grosvenor Sq. is shut up for the season. My home is quiet, orderly, and deeply satisfying after my long tumultuous winter in London and abroad. Every prospect opens to the future. Spring is making its first appearances in the fat bellies of ewes in my fields, and the first sprigs of wild corn are popping up in the fallow fields. It seems that my *escapade* with Fitzwm has gone entirely undetected, as Georgie never asks for information that I do not volunteer, and Gibson and Mrs. Reynolds hold their offices with saintly discretion. Fitzwm has returned to Gravesbrook to attend his family and make amends with his officers following this extended absence.

The contrast between the French and English modes of social ranking is stark, and I really believe that we have a beneficent system in place, so long as masters do not abuse their powers. Our critics call us a squirearchy, a swollen leech subsisting on the blood of rents and peerage lines. I wish to be the best landlord and the best master in England, as all good or ill is in my power to bestow. Why would I tend towards any evil, with such blessings following my full support? Why would I not assist my dependents in every endeavor, as their happiness is intimately linked to my own? Only when my subordinates behave badly towards me, do I find an outlet for my resentment in some penalty. That mischance happens so seldom – I can only recall Wickham's impertinence and later his outright villainy – and then an odd spot with an old tenant withholding rents that were in his power to pay. On the whole I am entirely sanguine about my position among the Lambton folk.

Georgie regaled me with sonatas from Beethoven and Haydn, and a well-behaved suite by Handel named after the harmonious blacksmith. She performed as beautifully as our old pianoforte could allow. She has played it so intensely this last year, I think she is nearly tickling the old baroque instrument into the floor. I told her of the pleasure I had in hearing a certain young lady in Hertfordshire play simple, folk airs, and Georgie promised to turn up those song-books as well, long buried in the years since our mother touched them. We shared a morning walk around the broad lake, where I described the London public balls and the fashions among ladies, as I supposed would be in the interest of a sixteen year old girl. She seemed little diverted by such descriptions, however, and she has always been shy in company. She asked with some apprehension whether I would expect her to come out next season. Especially after last year's misfortunes, I believe she is the one to decide when she chuses again to be out in male company.

Instead Georgie is interested in poetry, women's writing, and travel-logues from exotic locales, especially America and India. I shall infuse such riches into the library with a single letter to Johnson. My sister can read revolutionary texts the whole day through – who am I to limit her knowledge? I am done coddling and fathering. I wish to be a generous and open brother. I hinted to G that the Darcys might have some interest in America in coming generations, and that set her eyes flashing.

I dispatched a letter to Fitzwm at Gravesbrook requesting him to join me at Rosings in April. I require a man's company when it comes to the business of actually spending whole evenings at my Aunt's table beneath the lash of her tongue. Fitzwm knows well his duties to family, and I expect he will make the time, considering my labour in France on behalf of his friend.

My old pointer, Grin, is sprawled at my feet before the fire. He has not left my side the whole day long, except when Mrs. Reynolds put out his vittles at dark. He is eleven years, and gray about the muzzle, but his eyes are as clear as when he first led me in the hunts. Mrs. Reynolds tells me that Grin sired a litter of puppies with a local bulldog bitch, and their owner, the farmer Clay, has offered me the pick. I am trying to envision a pointer/bulldog chimera. Quite a monstrosity, I'd expect. The mutts will be ready for new homes in a week's time, and Georgie shall have her choice.

25 Feb   Pemberley

Ten paces between head and heart –

My head the mountain peak of noble thought;
my heart a harbour, cove, and hollow hide.
My head is smithy of ideas untaught;
my heart a pirate fleeing on the tide.
My head sees wealth and consequence as means;
my heart feels grace and quivers with it near.
My head courts two by two the social queens;
my heart is muted when she best could hear.

My head says "deduce," "truth," and "logically;"
my heart sighs "lovely," "lush," and "oh I wish!"
My head eats meat and vegetable and grain;
my heart drinks sweets and vine-born fruit and wine.
My head's a muscular, mailed, chilly fish
thrashing in my heart's shore-lost, raving sea.

1 March   Pemberley

The days pass rapidly and with leisure at once. I have been
relaxing, attending to one point of business at a time, and taking
care to be careful and deliberate. All of my rashness and
impatience has been assuaged in Paris. Now is for quiet, slow
time in wait for the fever of spring.

Gibson brought to my attention that gardener Sinclair has been
hatching a plan to improve pasture on the South fields by finding
the best combination of sweet grasses for ruminant fodder. What
follows sweet grass is happy animals, good milk and meat, and
low levels of disease and premature death. Gibson allotted ten
quid to build Sinclair a kind of experimental station for grasses.
It is comprised of some fifty raised beds, each containing a
unique combination of varieties. Like a chemist with his

bubbling flasks, each flask instead an engineered vat of earth, Sinclair selectively grazes animals on given plots to see their guttural response and the degree that the terrain resists heavy grazing. His hypothesis is that each species of plant does not operate in a vacuum, but relies intimately on the combination of species, their competition or cooperation with one another, and the manner of the soil in which they are planted. I had not before thought of the dirt as essential to the sweetness of my meat at table.

Though the experiment is only just started, Sinclair has great plans to manipulate his ranks through many permutations, and publish the results if he finds any germane information that would aid agriculture in the kingdom. Thus, at Pemberley we are at the forefront of knowledge in the natural sciences! Sinclair has left off his general gardening duties of trimming the topiary, clearing the arboretum floor, and sweeping the gravel paths.

When flower planting season is at hand, we will need recruits from the village to array Pemberley with her seasonal blooms. I have asked him to turn away from the formal geometric gardens and rather to dust the meadows with wildflower seeds, let the hedges roam and seedlings take root where acorns fall. Nature's patterns are best, though sometimes a gentle nudge from art aids in her array. I wish to complement last autumn's planting of ragged lanes of tulips and daffodils with whatever wildness introduces itself on the breeze. My loose mood will then be reflected in the living landscape, and thus the poet's habitat unites with the scientist's. Sinclair and his sons can always impose severe lines in future seasons, should I regain a fancy for Continental gardens.

9 Mar   Pemberley

I was strolling in a mist of thought towards Lambton on this chilly day, with the many schemes and hopes of my existence thrown in the air as juggling balls, and I kept as many of them under control as my mental powers allowed. From out the greensward came a family of gypsies, who had encamped in the shadows some hundred yards into the woods, led by two small children and their mother. The others held back as I was appealed by the first urchin to take interest in some of their peddler's wares. She held out, with a sweet smile, a raggedy soldier's uniform and a much-worn derby. The band were dirty, cold, and thin, but not threatening, and I paused for a moment to think over their plight. The gypsies have no protections from law, good employment, or society, and are the objects of universal censure and disparagement among more fortunate Englishmen, whether or not their conduct justifies the prejudice. They are undoubtedly of a different culture and bloodline – a pulse rather more lusty and mystical than ours, and an itinerant lifestyle. They are most often drawn to lives of entertainment in the circus, or they are drawn into crime, when they cannot persuade us to pay for their antics. As I had been thrashing about for God or the atom-universe to shift me in some good direction towards an answer for my love quandary, I suggested that one of them might sell me a divination. I was prepared to part with a few shillings for a fortune-tale.

The mother stepped forward immediately, and spoke in a broken French accent. "Tarot, monsieur. I read your future. Four shillings for Celtic cross." We agreed at two, for a simpler spread. Thus, I explain how I was swept from the public road through a sopping meadow to a leaky tent, and perched on a stool for fifteen minutes with a gypsy. No Englishman saw me stray into this alternate world, nor come back.

The lady of dark arts chanted many thick-tongued impressions of the cards laid before her, seven in a horse-shoe pattern, but I can recall few of her tales. As the mist and chill and heavy trees and spicy-smelling gypsies hung about, the whole atmosphere gave a heady sense of importance to the moment accompanied by an intoxicated imprecision of memory. I could not focus on her voice, only on the fabulous images on the cards. It was thus, in order of the seven cards: (past) the Tower upside down; (present) the Knave of Wands; (influences) the Lovers; (hurdles) the King of Swords; (hopes and fears) the Hanged Man; (course of action) the Star; and (resolution) the two of Chalices.

Each card got its own complex recitation, but I remember only the last words: "Your future may hold a full cup, monsieur, and a lady to drink with. See how you gaze in her eyes, if you but have the courage. The Lovers and the two Chalices go together; but the King of Swords can defeat all that comes after. Beware the warlord."

I paid her an added shilling for the pack itself, thanked her for her troubles, and proceeded to Lambton even more of a juggling clown afterwards than before. But it was a fine diversion, as complement to the auguries of religion and science.

15 Mar Pemberley

A Mr. Edward Webb and his assistant William Smith asked last week for the favour of meeting with me, and I acquiesced today. Gibson was at my side, sparkle-eyed, as they described their plans to open the interior of England to canals, and how these sluices would make my land twice as profitable and bring in prospectors for timber, coal, lead, and even fossils! I begged some time to think on the matter, and signed no waivers for him to conduct his surveys on my grounds. Demussy, he says, has already given him full access to his lands in return for a gratuity of twenty pounds. That sum should hold young Demussy afloat at the card-table in his club for another week.

In the private conference that followed, Gibson fervently advised that I allow them access to Pemberley estate, lest progress leaves me by the way-side, and canals are directed to enrich the commerce of neighboring farms. I require more time to consider.

21 Mar   Pemberley

Georgie and I seized this fine day, the first of Spring, and set out early on our annual circuit of the entire park – some twelve miles when we take the side-paths to the lagoon, the water-fall, and the bluff. Georgie wore her stoutest leather shoes and had her skirt rigged on a string to be lifted with ease, and I carried the knapsack of refreshments and dry clothes. We perceived some new evidence of drifters, as we found a recently used fire ring by the lagoon, in addition to the location where Sinclair found the vagrant soldiers. Our tree circle, first felled and excavated some nine years ago by Georgie, Wickham, and myself, is grown in with bramble, and I shall send up Sinclair's sons to clear it anew. Otherwise it was a pure, fine, serene, lovely day, open and free, in the company of my dear sister. She is endowed with the greatest gifts of body and mind – endurance, application, grace, and discretion. I trusted myself to name EB to her again, and how she is my model of an accomplished, savie modern woman. Georgie heard, smiled, and was silent. Even when we talk but little, we have the affinity of like souls.

I dined at supper with Georgie and Mrs. Annesley, who filled the table with her agreeable chatter and left us trail-worn travellers to our hearty plates.

24 Mar   Pemberley

Gibson asked me for an answer to Webb's request to survey my land for canals. The man has promised fifty pounds for the rights to make calculations, and Gibson is heavily in his favour, as he sees the future in the commerce of water-ways. Especially after my recent walk with Georgie that reinforced all my affection for the estate, with my brain bothered by the ricochet of imagined steam-engines clanging away at the soil, scooping it out in great ungodly heaps, I could not in the end acquiesce to Webb's designs. I have refused access for now. If I acquire Demussey's tracts, they may do their digging there.

By the time my son is old enough for college I expect he may propel his way up to Edinburgh or down to Cambridge on a steam-powered dingey.

28 Mar Pemberley woods

Sunrise earth: melting
the uplands to a fine mist
cupped in the valley

It is a Japanese form of poetry called the hokku. A sense impression – an image – then done. The above is mine; Georgie wrote the one below:

Sheep bahh cattle low
grass replies in silent green
electricity

29 Mar Pemberley

I have had a letter from Fitzwm, who will meet me in London and proceed together down to Kent in the course of a week or so. He needs that further time to arrange his absence with his family. Aunt Catherine several weeks ago sent her agreeable assent to our arrival, only wishing we could spare several months to celebrate the depth of our attachment to her domicile, herself, and her daughter.

I shall begin arrangements for my coming absence with Sutton, Gibson, and Mrs. Reynolds, who will have considerable business to attend at Pemberley this time of year.

Seeing her is so close I tremble with delightful fear.

5 April The Blue Boar Tavern, High Holborn

I have stopped only for the night in London on my way to Kent. I have business with Smithson on divers obligations, including the dispatch from Philadelphia that promises to report back on Monon by the end of summer, and the assets gathered to close with Demussy should he agree to my offer. I shall have to withdraw some of my investments in the China trade, but I am a soul more in love with land than capital, so it is no keen sacrifice. I also wanted Smithson's advice on Edward Webb's inquiries about canal-building in Derbyshire. Smithson says I am under no obligation to open my lands his surveying for these water-paths, but that my doing so might open my land to readier trade, and the harvesting of the forests. I shrink. It is rare that he and Gibson are united on the opposite side of my own inclinations.

Fitzwm will meet me at Grosvenor in the morning, and then we are off. I've spent so long anticipating my time with this mythical creature Elizabeth, and now the time draws near I find myself queasy at the thought of seeing her again. In the best case, she will disappoint me on second acquaintance. But there is a chance I will fall as much infatuated with her as I did last November, and then the pleasure of my regard will become at the price of decision. What would I sacrifice to have her? I wonder whether she really exists outside my overworked head.

I've drained two pints pondering this smoke-breathing she-dragon.

8 Apr   Rosings, Kent

After a little delay in London settling on Monon with sharp Smithson, Fitzwm and I arrived at Rosings this afternoon. I spent the evening saying as little as possible about my faux journey to Sheffield, and my mumblings about advances in the technology of steam engines fortunately offered so little prospect of colourful chatter for the ladies that my Aunt was obliged to engulph the remainder of the evening in her proclamations. Her tenants are scurrilous and lazy, and most likely Jacobins. Her servants are a cunning race that cheat her whenever she looses their chain. The French people are intoxicated with their strong wine and will wake tomorrow in the gutter, with all the heads of their most worthy masters piled about. The spring is late, and the hot-houses can barely hold all of the cucumbers and melons her Ladyship had the forethought to sow.

Aunt C allowed us to retreat to bed once we had delivered a full report of our own dissatisfactions with the world – a challenge for the affable Fitzwm – and I am fagged out and bewildered at once. She mentioned a pretty young friend of Mrs. Collins who is too decided in her opinions for one so young. Gentle sleep, nature's soft nurse, prepare me for the morrow and our reunion.

9 Apr   Rosings

We were regaled in the midst of breakfast by Mr. Collins, whose nose remained so close to the carpet I saw the freckles of his balding head more clearly than his lisping lips. He is unchanged by marriage, and even more insufferable in my Aunt's imperious company than he was whilst disgracing the Netherfield dance floor. No matter. His arrival gave us an excuse to call at Hunsford, and I have seen her. This day, I have laid my eyes on her. I promised myself to say very little, only to appear pleasant and in command. I enquired about her family, and was reminded of the pleasant melody of her voice. Made stupid by this reverie,

I heard not what she actually said, until I came back to my mind by her direct query on my seeing her sister in London. Another falsehood left my lips – though a necessary one – I claimed complete ignorance, and felt more acutely the shame of lying than I ever had before.

She is unchanged – that is, dreadfully alluring!

Fitzwm was completely charmed by Eliza as well, and came away full of her. I had to suffer my dear cousin's admiration of her face and figure without hardly trusting myself to agree. How deceitful I have become to everyone – friends, family, close and remote! How many confessions I shall have to make if I chuse her. So, the trial is begun.

15 Apr   Rosings

Damn my Aunt's demands on my time! I have this week had no time for any business but hers. I have visited every one of her tenants and observed her scolding manner with them. I smoothed some of the relations by suggesting how an investment in the repair of several farms would actually help my Aunt's returns. She is instinctually cheap. She expects to shake manna out of the tatters of her husband's small investments dating from the 1780s! I dedicated my week to drawing up close plans as to the potential improvement of each farm (some twelve in total), and have gained the assent of most tenants to my proposals. The major improvements revolve around irrigation and investment in seed stock. The buildings themselves are sound, as my Aunt will not tolerate a sloppy structure polluting her domain, and her tenants frequently invest more of their labour and small cash in repairs and prettying than in the business of farming. They are overjoyed to have anyone pay sympathy to their travails. The sharper task has been to convince my Aunt that only by opening her purse may money find ingress. She looked on the business with much more favour when I hinted as to how I would like my farms to operate, were I to become Landlord in the parish.

I have borne the company of Mr. Collins for many of these visits. His wishes to coach and coax his raggedy flock into complete submission to their Mistress, so he takes it upon himself to visit not only on behalf of the Deity he deigns to represent, but on behalf of that more formidable higher power who pays his grocery bills. He has a little recitation for each farmer, repeating his dictates of how their agrarian fortunes represent the favour or disfavour of God upon their work; the inheritance of the lowly office as peddlers in dirt and dung requires them to be completely selfless and beyond any regard of weakness or physical fatigue, which again, would recycle back to the disfavour of God were they to slacken for even two breaths together. Quite out of breath himself, he then helps himself to their largest chair and puffs and simpers about deference to rank and the beneficence of her awful Ladyship. The poor farmer's wife relieves him with fresh milk or, when available, tea and sugar and cake and currants. You must learn by my example, he says, and live in severe modesty, for your gifts may come in a later life, should God judge you worthy.

Only after Mr. Collins has performed his Supreme dictates have I any time to discuss the real business of the farm and the penury of its circumstances. I have actually sent Collins away on several occasions in order to clear space for the farmer to be honest about his privations. It is little wonder that the crop failures have figured more severely on my Aunt's lands, which only fuels her anger at the increases in land tax in Kent. She has refused to support the purchase of new seed upon crop failures, has resisted any improvements in irrigation despite the remoteness of her lands from rivers and bog lands. Yet she expects a continual flow of compliments in the form of legs of lamb, eggs, milk, vegetables, and orchard fruits. One young farmer, Dunder, told me that my Aunt had ordered his ancient ailing father to be loaded onto a hay-cart bound for the next parish, so she would not have to pay his funeral expenses. So may the most neglectful gentry, like the alchemists, render gold from base mentalities, and marvel at their genius through long idle afternoons!

My other prescribed task has been to comb through the library at Rosings to identify any revolutionary texts than might be polluting my Aunt's collection. My uncle had such a conservative taste, completely unreformed by his widow in the last twelve years, that the only spark on the shelf was Bentham's *Principles of Legislation*, and a picture book of Michelangelo's nude sketches. I will keep those for Pemberley and would set fire to the rest were it mine to dispose. My Aunt was pacified with the removal of the two dangerous tomes. Edmund Burke now reigns supreme.

My cousin Fitzwm has borne none of these tasks, as my Aunt considers military men completely inept with domestic economy. Thus dismissed with the wave of her hand, he has cheerily called nearly every day at Hunsford to meet with the ladies there, the sly jack, when I am claimed by my Aunt before breakfast. I am teazed by his innocent admirations. At least this long week has given me the chance to do some good among my Aunt's tenants, which may partway make up for her long standing neglect. And it has given me time to settle my mind to the purpose at hand.

16 Apr   (Easter Day)   Rosings

At last I have enjoyed her company. This is the first time I have had the chance to regard her since the day after my arrival. We walked side-by-side from my Aunt's table to her sitting room, and as I felt so much, alas I could think of nothing to say. My Aunt has a large gaudy mirror placed over the great hearth in her sitting room. At our evening gathering following supper, I made a study of the world as it is, and then of the reflected world within the mirror where everything is reversed. Instead of being expected to join in marriage with Anne, in the mirror world Elizabeth was my bride, and we were visiting my Aunt and cousin in a familial way. Though the room's real inhabitants were prim, stuffy, and self-important (Eliza and Fitzwm excepted), in the mirror world everyone was charming. My Aunt was amusing and generous-minded, my cousin glowing in health and worldly opinions, and I was easy and open, happy in the company of a beloved wife.

I confess that I missed half the *real* conversation by gazing in the mirror at Elizabeth's reflection, and the line from her chin down her soft throat to her lace bodice, worn low in the warm spring weather. Though she seemed unknowing of my regard, her friend Mrs. Collins several times met my eye with a look of curiosity. She is on to me. I was called back to reality by my Aunt's repeated queries about my sister, her pianoforte, and my health. She feigned concern that I ate not enough at supper. My stomach is queasy at the scent of any food, excepting Eliza.

Fitzwm persuaded her to play for our party, and she delightfully sang a new folk air "Flow Gently, Sweet Afton," from the Scottish poet Burns. It is a pastoral love song. "How wanton thy waters her snowy feet lave…". My cousin and I stood enraptured, until Eliza met my eye and teazed me for standing like a stock solider to the loose organic flow of the song's verses. She vowed not to be frightened, and exercised her nerve by calling me out to my cousin in reporting on my behaviour at Hertfordshire last November. What an image she painted! I succeeded, it seems, in covering my extraordinary regard for her at Netherfield. I justified the ways of Darcy to strange ladies by pointing out my native shyness, a trait that cannot be despised, though it may be censured by the easily sociable. It was easier to engage her when Fitzwm was standing by as her interlocutor –

she spoke to *me* through him. My best answers came in the form of smiles, which flowed freely with her succession of songs at the piano. When the carriage swept her away, the instrument yet resonated in my mind, in harmony with my resolve to have her.

We have similar minds, borne on different dispositions. Neither of us perform for strangers, and our powers to please fall only on the worthy. Yet she might soften me, and coax the man inside from the shell of the gentleman I present to the world.

My fantasy of the mirror and the piano, the pleasures of this sublime evening – all may be mine. I may have her if I but have the nerve to chuse her. Why would I, a man of privilege and freedom, be made miserable by outside expectations? What is the advantage of wealth if I may not be free to live in the way that makes me happy? Expectations are all the more suffocating when one's soul cries out against them. The rose is ready to pluck, thorns and red petals all.

Heaven help me, my choice is made. My name for her caress. I shall kiss her fingers one by one. We shall cross the world together, or chuse to leave it unseen.

17 Apr   Rosings

This morning I was elated by the scud of a letter underneath my bedroom door. It came not from lover nor friend, but from cousin Anne, who to my infinite surprise is horrified by her mother's evangelism on her behalf. Anne writes in secresy to beg my forbearance. She writes – begging all the while not to offend me -- that she does not share her mother's hopes for our betrothal because she does not mean to marry at all. She is mortally afraid of child bearing. Anne can think of nothing more terrifying than the prospect of giving birth and suckling a babe when she can hardly walk out of doors for a quarter of an hour. She asks me merely to keep her comfortable after the death of her mother (should she outlive her mother) and not remove her from Rosings or the gentle care of dear Mrs. Jenkinson. It is no wonder, considering her ill health that her many doctors have failed to renew. She begs me never to propose to her, to resist her mother's demands, and instead to chuse a woman who pleases me.

I do not know what to think, except to feel relief that my escape will offend only one, not two, of my close relations. We have been weird since childhood, she so frail and stilted in her mother's presence and yet supposed to be the object of my affection. Now I begin to suspect that my cousin has an entire other life outside the purview of her mother. Anne is perfectly aware that I will inherit Rosings and the estate upon Aunt C's death – my being the nearest and eldest male relation – and while her mother is determined to have her own offspring as mother to the next generation of Rosings' proprietors, the supposed bride herself sets me free! I still have the more formidable Matron to inform of the change.

I suspect there is more at play here than my cousin's morbid fear of parturition. She has occasionally sent me letters inquiring about the learned ladies' events in London, and begged me to send her confidential packets of pamphlets and articles arguing for the rights of women. I am only too sympathetic to their ideas, and cannot but think that Anne is a closet Blue Stocking. Despite her conservatism, Aunt Catherine believes in the power of the reasoning female. If Anne has been entirely secretive about her reading – sharing it perhaps only with Mrs. Jenkinson – I shall encourage her to become more forthright with her mother. The twenties are the age to starch up the spine a bit and confront one's parents. She might find her mother more sanguine than she expects, and it may be in my power to enlarge the Rosings library with strategic gifts that would please both mother and daughter.

The truth and proof of my liberation lies in the fact that Anne wishes not to marry, but would not have the strength to reject me should I make the long-awaited offer. It is admirable. The timing is most wonderfully aligned with my own inclinations elsewhere. I have burnt her letter, and wrote to Johnson in London to acquire me a new imprint of Lady Mary Montagu's letters from Turkey, which I will make up as a present for my dear cousin.

As soon as I had a moment alone with Anne before supper, I kissed her hand with warmth and thanked her from my soul for her honest communication. She is a good girl. She expressed her desire to see me happy and liberal with my affection, and said that sickly ladies are best off with books and ideas, not dwelling in the tiresome fleshy world of wives and mothers.

20 Apr   Rosings

For each of the last three days I have taken long walks in the park in the most beautiful of verdant Eastertide. Everything is growing to fruition in the full organic splendour of spring. I have been mulling over my reasons, needs, and affections, my duties to family and propriety, and my desires as a man. Sometimes Fitzwm joins me, though there is an embargo on how forthright I can be with him. We have at length discussed the expectations of a first born son versus a younger one. He convinces me, not knowing this conviction's end, that eldest sons actually have the greatest freedom to chuse a wife, because they have estates and wealth assured and need not marry in pursuit of material comfort. He scoffs at my contrary view. He even mentioned his attraction to Eliza, and how a woman of her spirit would be the wife of his choice, but sadly he must chuse where prudence dictates rather than where affection lights. I nearly shook my hat off when he named her as his choice by inclination – though undetected. Our minds are full of the same woman, which makes my dear cousin for once a most tormenting companion.

Other times I walk alone, bewildered on the shores of this irrevocable decision. I visit the farms and assist in what ways I might – with little favours of fruits and nuts from my Aunt's table – I play with the local children and envision the fresh faces of my own unborn children. Will they have bright eyes and long lashes? What raptures in their begetting?

Each day in the full of morning I turn my steps towards the lane that runs beside the main road, where I may find Eliza on her daily stroll. If I find her not out of doors, I gather the courage to call at the house. We share a half an hour together, sometimes alone, as I ask her questions about her inclinations to marry, to settle, about her attachment to family and to Hertfordshire. Her answers are pleasing. She expresses no desire to stay close to home. She prizes affection rather than convenience, with a penetrating apprehension that has perfectly captured the marriage of her friend to the ass Collins. She has become less saucy with me, and more comfortable. We are friends.

I described my travels to Italy and Greece, and how my skin browned and filled me with lassitude in those hot climates. In Hunsford house she is staying in a chilly north-facing room that fronts on the road, and we talked of the strong melancholic effects of a lack of sunshine. She walks each day so as to avoid Collins in his garden, but to share in the salubrious fresh air. Less guarded now than I ever have been, I said she shall enjoy the sunny prospect of the south-west windows on the second floor at Rosings, which look out over a few acres of wild copse that my Aunt has allowed to remain in consideration of the rabbit-holes, pheasant roosts, and fox-dens in refuge there. She lightly replied she would take my word as gospel, since she never expects to travel abroad nor sleep under the august roof of my Aunt, and that it was cruel for me to teaze her with scenes that neither her sex nor her situation in life would allow her to enjoy. There was just such an uncertain emphasis behind her words that I left off the matter there.

She can no longer have any confusion about my interest, though she may yet be unaware of the depth of my yearning. It does not diminish with further contact, as I had believed it might. She has energy, brightness, courage, kindness, and great intellectual gifts. She is uniquely beautiful. I must constantly remind myself not to take her hand or reach for her waist as we walk. Each night as I lie awake in bed I replay the conversation, study it and point to its features like a king's cartographer studies an exotic new colony. I memorize my lines before the next day's encounter in case my shyness overwhelms me. Each day I grow more natural in her company, and our conversations thus spontaneous.

My reason and my feelings have weighed on opposite scales, and Fitzwm and Anne have unknowingly removed a few iron bars from the weight of reason against a proposal. Eliza has for her part added gold bars to the weight of my feelings. I need only the courage to act. I have resisted the utmost force of this passion to the best of my ability, and have not the will to suppress it further. My regard for her has been at banquet these five days. Now I wish only to have and hold her, and close my eyes to sneering scruples.

I shall ride tomorrow to London to purchase a ring. My excuse shall be the new pianoforte I have long meant to send up to Pemberley for my sister's pleasure.

23 Apr   Rosings

Today is the day. I have been to Church with my Aunt and I paid especial homage to the chief Titan who giveth and taketh away, by mortifying my knees in extended prayer. I mumbled many "pleases" and "if it be your will," but I still think, secret diary, it is rather *my* will that is the engine of this proposal, and *my* desire the furnace that drives it down the line. Alas, I fear I failed in the office of humble supplication – my mind is not formed to be a penitent man. As He made me, I expect His confidence in me will not go unrewarded.

The ring I bought is rare American gold from the state of North Carolina, rather than the abundant stores melted down from disbanded French collections. I found the ring I wanted at a stall in the Western Exchange in Bond Street. I wandered as in a dream through the Pantheon, along Pall Mall and over to Bond Street, where I alighted on my choice. Mr. Burton, the shop keeper, assured me that the era of American gold is dawning, and I received a certificate of authenticity that mark this ring as among the first to reach England. It may become a symbol of our future lives together, should she wish to make a life in the New World. Monon or Pemberley – I will live in happiness wherever her inclinations bend. Burton will fit the ring with a diamond selected by my bride when we first travel to London together. I spent half the ride back in silly fancies about the lost Louis Blue Diamond, the symbol of the Golden Fleece that has been missing since 1792, and whether it might turn up in time for our wedding. The London jewelers are flooded with French diamonds, stolen and hacked from the ladies' large collections, but Burton said the best new gems are coming in from Brazil.

Georgie's pianoforte was less difficult to find than the gold ring – I made purchase of Broadwood's finest six octave instrument inlaid with ivory and ebony in an japanned pattern, and arranged for it to be sent up with great care to Derbyshire. He assured its arrival by midsummer.

Diary, wish me luck! I am shaking with – I know not what – fear, folly, delight, anticipation. She comes to tea at Rosings this evening, where after I might claim a moment alone to walk her back to Hunsford. I must maintain reason as I present my proposal, and not have my feelings run away with me as a fool might. She is a rational creature and will wish to be informed of the family obstacles that have long prevented my forming a serious design on her, and that the degradation that I might well feel in making an inferior alliance is nothing compared to my ardent love for her. I have drafted my speech, and once the queasy business is covered, we may simply enjoy the prospect of our lives together. What splendid increase in her fortunes will accompany my avowal!

Will the promise from her lips recover me from this insanity, or drive me deeper? What does she smell like, feel like, taste like? What doors of exstatic perception will she throw open? I am at a crossroads, and I feel the rigid conformity of my former life slipping away under the surge of a brave new era of liberality, joy, exploration. Yet stay sober for the proposal!

24 Apr   Rosings

All is lost. I cannot write. I have written at a letter all night. I am a pebble cast in the ocean.

As flies to wanton boys, are we to Gods. They kill us for their sport.

26 Apr   Grosvenor Square

I now feel equal to some confession, less angry, less bewildered. She will not have me. She thinks me a snob, a blackguard, a malicious advisor to friends, a relentless villain to enemies. She thinks me not a gentleman, me not worthy of *her*. I am rejected.

I had been up all night after her rejection writing a letter redressing her counts against me. I delivered it to her hands yesterday morning, without a further word but a touch of my *chapeau.* She looked weary and red-eyed, but yet defiant. I hardly cut a fine figure, wandering the misty glen in hopes of accosting her. She is misinformed on some details, especially as regards my history with Wickham. But she is dreadfully correct about aspects of my conduct. Only now I begin to see.

The mode of her rejection was exactly calculated to make me understand the depth of my wishes. Never have I so honestly felt that I loved her, when all love must be in vain. I knew not what to do but flee with petty and obscure excuses to my relations.

I confessed the whole of it to Fitzwm in the carriage to London. I cried to him. He only listened in astonishment, and offered no advice but his sympathy.

3 May   The Brown Beagle Inn   Leicestershire

I parted with Fitzwm two days ago. He was still amazed at my intelligence, never having suspected the depth of my regard for EB, never having any idea that I would look on her as a woman of my peerage. How little everyone knows me! Even my closest friends and family. It is my own burden to bear. I am to blame. Fitzwm left me as requested and remained in London to fix up some of our business there. Anne is relieved not to have an offer from me, and her mother sits complacent on her pile of fantasies. She is no more deluded about the world than I have been.

I have stopped at a non-descript inn most of the way back to Pemberley from London. I will rest here another night and try to gather my spirits before seeing Georgianna. Now the beauty of the weather, the warm breezes and dappled shades of the highway, the laughter of the folk emerging from winter, the active animals, the tender leaves, everything is torment. Cruel lashing torment.

Had I behaved in a more gentleman-like manner! Had I behaved in a more *human*-like manner. Had I behaved as though blood were in my heart rather than glacial melt. Had I taken Bingley's good example and engaged in idle *repartée* with good humour. Had I a thought cross my lips without constant deference to rank and fortune. Had I expressed my deep regard for her alone as the reason for her to be my wife, and left my misgivings silent. Had I laughed at my nagging obligations to society. Had I treated Bingley with more respect for his deep regard for Jane Bennet. Had I shared my humble concerns with Bingley about Miss Bennet's heart rather than assuring him that her regard was non-existent. Had I stopped to consider the personal and general danger of imagining everyone as pawns beneath my sceptre.

Had I respected my father's wishes to see Wickham well looked after. Had I been patient and sympathetic to the whims and caprice of a young man whose living could be assured only by my liberal actions. Had I exerted myself to find another position for the man who was my playmate in childhood. Had I been less prone to seeing only the wicked in Wickham. Had I not been such an execrable prude on every occasion where amiability can oil the intercourse of society. Had I the last half-year to live over again!

Bar wench, another pint of ale for this miserable pauper, this grub-worm, this booby, this nincompoop.

15 May   Pemberley

I have passed an eternal fortnight and am awarded with some greater understanding of my headlong errors, that I may never commit them again.

I have found fruit in dwelling upon my past mistakes and observing the trends that have placed me in this tormented situation. Though an observer might award justice to EB's accusations about my conduct towards Bingley, but find mere misinformation and error in her accusations regarding Wickham, I have begun to see the two cases as intimately related. Both unhappy results can be understood through my ill conduct. Both grow out of my wrong-headed assumption that I can manipulate others without impacting myself, and that I have superior knowledge about what is right for them. Not only could I have assured Wickham a living that would suit him using the ample resources of Pemberley – after all, I would not wish to be conscribed to the clergy, nor to law – I could easily have taken a more sympathetic view of his conduct towards Georgianna.

Yes – even that! Georgie's misery this past year has been due to embarrassment in disappointing me, to be sure, but more relevantly her misery stems from sheer loneliness and desire for affection. Wickham is a warm and affectionate man, and I now believe that he did love her. My pride screamed that he ran away with my sister to chagrin myself, and with the most pusillanimous and dodgey motives of avarice, but I have been forced to recall the moments of true regard shared between them. There is no doubt that their match would have been surprising and in some ways imprudent. But any more so than my alliance with EB? He is an honourary son of my father, and a man of considerable charm and capability. Georgie was not of age and I had the power, as guardian, to forbid the match. Power should be used lightly, and with beneficence. I dismissed him with too much venom. Would I had heard his case, heard her own expressions of affection! Perhaps they could have courted for some months or years, and gone with open eyes into a marriage, in due time. It is exactly the kind of capricious and despotic power over others that Godwin admonishes in Caleb Williams.

When Wickham accosted me on his horse in Meryton, I saw only the villain who meant to despoil my sister. I saw not the disappointed lover who had cared for Georgie since birth.

Though I cannot entirely excuse his conduct in this matter, I must acknowledge how my own behaviour has fed the flames of his revenge. I could even have helped stem his vicious propensities to drink and gamble had I engaged in true and open friendship with him in college. My pride and sense of superiority have weaved this trap in which I find myself flailing. EB is right even where she is wrong.

And, of course, she is right where she is right. With Bingley I have no excuses. The excuses I have made for my conduct are hollow. His misery last Christmas is on my head. I allowed Caroline to influence me, and I allowed my own fear of my regard for EB and my squeamishness about her family to selfishly disfavour Bingley's affections. Could it have been done to a more deserving creature than Bingley? Might the death of his friend Mayor have been softened by his betrothal to a lovely and worthy woman?

In the light of these two cases, where does the difference lie? I have ruined the happiness of two couples, four individuals who, if not all right-worthy in their behaviour, might have been brought into a sphere of grace given the proper notice and respect. Yes, even Wickham brought into the Darcy circle might have made an admirable, energetic, and affectionate brother. What of his father, the good steward? Old Wickham, may he rest in peace, would hate me for what I've reaped with his son. Could I have behaved the same way had he been living, or my father?

It is like this: I am perfectly amiable with those of obviously lower rank – my tenants, those in my employ like Mrs. Reynolds, Mrs. Annesley, and Sutton. But where the line blurs, as with an honourary son like Wickham, or a lower gentle family like the Bennets, or a family wealthy by trade like the Bingleys, I become high-handed to protect my sense of superiority. In this I am hardly different from my Aunt, who requires any slight distinction of rank to be preserved. Until this moment, I never knew myself. I have played the part of the tragic hero, destined by his ego to fall into *hamartia*. I shall make changes. Here follows the *peripeteia*, and the future is open. I wish to be Benedick, not Coriolanus. I shall change my life.

18 May   Pemberley

I am acting upon my good resolve. I have written to Bingley in London begging him to set aside a fortnight in July to join me at Pemberley, promising all the allure of midsummer at the deer park and trout stream. More to the point, we may have an honest exchange redressing my past misconduct. I shall explain my gruesome behaviour and release him to the pleasure of courting Jane Bennet if he should chuse her. Should my machinations be reversed, Caroline will learn that her influence over my actions is but temporary. She shall think I invite her brother hither to expose him to Georgie's charms, but that misimpression I cannot avoid. A woman's match-making mind is a cluttered closet I shall not enter.

Will I ever see EB again, or is she past recovery, destined to live outside the circle of my arms? Does she believe my letter, or does its bitterness redouble her dislike?

I have been poring over de Warville's narrative of New Travels in America, sent ahead to me by Johnson. Warville details plans for emigration. I was particularly struck by his approach to Philadelphia, on "a fine road bordered by the best cultivated fields, and elegant houses, which announce the neighborhood of a great town." He admires the Society of Friends, the Quakers, for their humble nobility and self-sufficiency. Their milk is sweet, their grain fat and un-mouldered, and their community perfectly designed to exact happiness from a life of reasonable labour. When I think of the excesses and degradations of

London! The hypocritical penury of the Anglican leaders, who snorfle at noble pockets lined with riches! The lisping ladies and fat indolent rakes of high society! And the fatuous Prince Regent, ringleader and laughing stock of them all! How might we gentry recover our pride, our dignity, our right to lead the nation with proper merit and wise beneficence? I begin to think the *bourgeois* class is our best hope for social improvement, but that they so often model their behaviours upon the worst of our own.

I spent two full hours in the arboretum with Mrs. Bursted's largest iron pan – ten quarts! I am quite fainting with manliness.

21 May   Pemberley

One sonnet will starve it entirely away…

> God, or some force of nature, give me strength
> to rise again, and plant the furrowed corn.
> Entrust that tender sprouts again are born
> to live hot daytimes stretching to their length.
> Wealth, or some higher form of valor, fill
> my impoverished husk of heart with blood.
> Courageous may I wrestle with this drudge,
> grow lordly careless of desires unkilled.
> Reason, or some creative frame of mind,
> instruct me in the calculus of stars,
> amuse the moon with rhymes that praise her scars,
> flash on me infinity till I'm blind.
> But tho' I strain as Atlas with his planet,
> the galaxies yet resolve upon Miss Bennet.

29 May   Pemberley

I long to be alone, to grieve and heal alone, to meditate on my condition and discover some reason to live and be happy in this dreadful condition of heartache. I shall become a vagrant on my own property. I shall escape to America once Georgie is well married. I have arranged for her to spend a week with her friend Miss Fitzpatrick, whose family lives in Nottingham. I've told Gibson to make my excuses to the community for a few days' time so I may take leave of my proper self.

I shall sleep under the leaves and stars, as the evenings grow fine and my sad heart keens in my chest. There is an actual spot that hurts – I had never felt it before – it lies in the exact middle of my chest, just where the ribs part at the top of the stomach. I feel my sick soul.

My bride shall be night. I have put away some coarse bread, cheese, salt pork, and carrots. I shall drink water from the creek. I will also pack that half-bottle of laudanum to release my imagination to its supernatural devices. It will either plunge me into the presence of she who torments me, so I may drown in pleasure and wake a new man, or the opiate will render this whole business so hideous to my mind that I cannot dwell upon it longer. You, dear diary, will receive the faithful account of what happens to Darcy in the wild.

30 May   Pemberley woods

It is a damned uncomfortable thing sleeping on the damp ground. That is my first learning. I am Rousseau's wild man, purifying myself from the dregs of society and sitting atop this prospect without a view of dominion (though it is my land), but a view that shows my terrifying smallness in the realm of the peaks. Not only am I small in body, but in time I am a lamp's flicker upon the great trance of the stars. I am humbled by its grandeur. Already I simply exist more; I find myself less angry, less impatient, less helplessly depressed. I find myself healthy in exhaustion – and would sleep an age *en plein air*. Now for the brain-show of dazzling sublime. I measure my dose.

1 June   Pemberley woods

Though still far from sober, let me *essai*, and compose some of the wild apparitions and encounters of last night and the turns of the morning. I took a dozen drops of the anodyne at sunset, having napped much of the sunny afternoon and feeling refreshed. For a meditative sun-fall I existed as a tree, feeling every breeze and atom of sunlight on my skin, watching the scenes near and far, from the smallest mote at my feet to the far views beyond Lambton where the hills rise in jagged gestures off towards Mam Tor. The landscape of rocks seemed peopled with the Titans, those lost gods of Grecian lore.

I lived in slow time, and the interconnexion between me and the earth was absolute. My lungs were leaves, my brain the stream at my back, the hills bones of my long-sleeping body. I was eternal, but not as me, the tyrannical I, but all-encompass, like a global machine that was both in me and I was a part within it. Not just Darcy, but something else was looking through my eyes and coaching me on greater awareness of perception. Quotidian splintered. This second I, the laudanum self, extended space out to universal, time to eternal. My rational self says I took drops about fourteen hours ago, but subjectively it has been aeons. These summer days are long by the clock, and this one day and night has made me a happy old sage inside. I wonder if my next encounter with a mirror will reveal a web of smile lines.

At long last the old sun fell down and left me in darkness close with the trees. I got up to stretch my legs and floated along hill paths until I arrived at the old tree circle cleared by Georgie, Wickham, and myself some years ago. It is a circle twenty feet wide surrounded by a close fence of birches, with a fire pit in the midst. Sinclair's sons have recently cleared it at my behest. From this great chimney of trunks arose a fire I must have lit and all the illuminated trunks took on appearances called up from my mind. Some threatening, like a ghost of sneering Aunt Catherine in a knotty old birch, some sorrowful, like Jane Bennet's downcast face behind waving leaves – but as each impression came I saw and acknowledged it, and it dwelled as long as I wished it to. I fancy I had a conversation with young Wickham, the better younger boy; I fancy I consoled with Jane about her sadness and was sorry for my part in it. Anne emanated from a solid oak façade and heaped wood on my fire. The redoubled fire brought a healthy glow to her face, and we held hands as we were children again. The glowing coals themselves were companions. Once I greeted the apparitions, they were my friends, no threat to me. Justine emerged from the shadows and kissed me deeply, then she fell away laughing into the fire. Sabine came and curtseyed prettily, calling me *l'oncle Anglais* she sat on my knee for a while before she skipped off into the darkness.

Feeling the command I had, I invoked EB to join me, and before long she came on silent feet and sat at my right hand, taking it up and putting my palm to her lips. We spent years together last night, yet I recall nothing said, only her presence filled me with penitence and fervour. She was not angry. She had in her eyes the gladness of all women ever loved, and the glimmer absolved my pride and kept me entranced in the joy of being alive. She came and remained. Her skirts absorbed the tears of joy and relief that came unbidden to my eyes.

With each of these apparitions, I was in full knowledge of their fiction, even as I fancied the encounter. It was not as the hallucinations of a lunatic, who believes in the truth of his deranged mind; no, instead I was consciously leading myself through a series of fantasies, as in a lucid dream. Though laudanum oft results in horror and trepidation, this night it has been a gentle, generous guide towards redemption; it has opened the vast internal space of self-awareness. I am enlarged on the inside. I must not forget what I have known here.

2 June   Pemberley woods

Here I sit in a pose like an Eastern sage, a Buddou, quite content alone but full of the love of others, leaf-broken sunlight on my face, at last in a mood of gratefulness that I have not felt for many years. I have traversed the dark places. I owe to Elizabeth the restoration of my humanity, and will be a better man, and gentleman, for her acquaintance. That she even exists is a blessing. That I may not have her is a lesson in the limits of this lifetime – I of all privileged men cannot simply lay my hand on any girl and call her my property – there is justice in it. Though I ache for her still, I have some peace at last. Thinking myself entitled to the favour of any maid simply because of my rank is the kind of odious *hauteur* I've learned from Aunt Catherine and my mother before her. Elizabeth is a woman truly worth pleasing, and if the gods please I will take pleasure in pleasing her when we meet again. If I am blessed enough to meet her again.

Here is what I've discovered whilst sitting in Pemberley woods: I was attached to Elizabeth by way of possession. I wanted her body, her mind, her esprit, to call my own property. The law supports me in that absurd declaration! But she is not to be possessed; I am only to suffering an attachment to the idea of her as a parcel of woman, fenced in and dispatched at will like a standing reserve of timber. Instead, I have found happiness in the spots of breath, of clarity, of release from resentment, not in having but in being. I am aware enough to let go of the past and dismiss the tyranny of a pessimistic future. Nostalgia, farewell. Augury, adieu! Today, this moment, is my dominion, and Elizabeth breathes free somewhere in the Kingdom. I wish her well. I owe so much to her already. I am a fuller man now, freer to express my generous self. In proposing to her I was true to my feelings, but dead wrong in my order of values.

The anodyne has helped me dismiss that haunting memory of her rejection, the dismissive sparring, the precise terms of her dislike as she articulated them. Instead I was able to reinvent our relationship on a landscape of understanding and sympathy. I know it was all in my mind – that wilderness of dreams is exactly the sort of derangement that figures enlightenment. Though I may still be a fool, I do wholly believe that if I am right-worthy in my behaviour, the fates will give me another chance to change her view of me. I must not throw myself in her path and beg for audience; I must have faith that the sheer gravity of my regard will draw her back for another look. Wise passiveness! I need only one more chance. Last night my heart whispered that anything is possible.

I have one dread that I cannot destroy: the news that she is engaged to another man. It may come someday. It is one remnant of the possessive nature that I have not yet tamed.

10 June   Pemberley

Diary, forgive my lassitude. I wander still within a dream, waiting for some impulse to spur me into my future life. What it holds I cannot imagine. The world figures me master of a dominion. In truth I can hardly master myself. I am at peace only in the present.

Summer begins, and I am busy with my tenants, making my rounds and agreeing to plans for improvements. The farms run by Rust, Martin, Jenkins, and Dunston shall be expanded by clearing the wastes of gorse and bracken. I have hired all the idle Lambton boys over the age of twelve to help the farmers, and three girls not yet married have accepted the work as well. They hope to clear eight waste acres by the new moon (some two weeks hence). I will finance the well dressing at Lambton, as usual, and the villagers have decided upon a Georgian theme to celebrate our bountiful harvest of last year – and this?

I have received an invitation from John Paterson, the clerk of works at the University of Edinburgh, to join him in a personal tour of their new constructions that aim to make regular the plans of the Old College. He promises fine company among the medical professors, tender meals and sound vintages – the standard treatment for walking cheque-books such as myself. I am at leisure. I shall leave in two days, to arrive in a fortnight.

16 June   Rose & Crown Inn, Carlisle

We are traveling by barouche to Scotland – I have brought Georgie and Mrs. Annesley for their pleasure and to keep me from brooding – and we rolled through scene after scene of varied delight. Georgie brought her Claude glass, and, half-joking, framed every new vista from the carriage window and bubbled her exstacies with the picturesque. Mrs. Annesley helps along her theories by reading passages of Gilpin that speak to the scenes. Georgie is quite talkative in our familiar company, and I am gratified to find her artlessly happy this summer. We, both of us, are coming along in our recovery from past misconduct.

I remember EB jibing at the picturesque whilst we walked the paths of Netherfield last winter. Rather than bar her from my thoughts, I welcome her spirit into my notice, as I guess at what sharp and playful remark she might have inserted into Georgie's exstacies. We travelled from Matlock through the Peaks to Buxton, skirted Manchester and Preston, then plunged through the Lake District, where we bid Bateson to pause most often under the gaze of Georgie's glass. She took sketches of several scenes that she means to finish in the dull times at Pemberley. We spent the whole of yesterday afternoon lazing in the shade of the imperial elms on the shores of Esthwaite, quite useless to the peevish world beyond our happy indolent little sphere. We stayed at Hawkshead. The sway of elms and rippling glacier lakes, the simple pleasant yeomen and wandering poets, the scene recovers me.

To-night we mean to dine at Carlisle castle, and visit the historical sites of the Jacobins and Bonnie Prince Charlie – so off with me thither.

19 June   The White Hart Inn, Edinburgh

Perhaps Paterson despaired of my ever arriving, but when our carriage with the Darcy crest rolled up to the door, spattered in mud, squeaking from the rutted road, we were well-attended. Depositing the ladies to a front room at the inn, which commands a view of the Grassmarket, Paterson was rather horrified at my choice of the locale, Grassmarket being a poorer part of town, but Georgie wished to see the horse and cattle exchanges, and it is close to Edinburgh Castle. Indeed there is a constant din of neighing, lowing, and bidding in the background, and the square is paved with dung. For her innocence I only hope there are no executions planned for the next three days.

The ladies will be attended by Paterson's wife and a male escort around town, and I am soon to be swept up into the business of the languishing university architecture.

22 June   The White Hart Inn, Edinburgh

I have been tutored on new electrical theories of the body's animation, I have witnessed wine-soaked debates between materialists and vitalists, I have applied my mind to the complexities of epigenesis and spiritual evolution, I have toured the Royal Infirmary Inn at High School Yards (a measly small facility), I have witnessed internal surgery in the theatre and watched the agonies of the living patient under the work of eminent sawbones, I have seen a baby born to an audience of three score medical students, I have seen an old man pass off with only a doctor, a deacon, and myself to bid him adieu.

With such a bracing tour of modern medicine, I left Paterson with a personal investment of £500 to be paid out in an annuity over the course of ten years. It will be used in assistance of his new plan for the university's new buildings. Work has been largely suspended for these five years due to the loss of public funds with the wars abroad, though he did with relish show me the six massive columns he has erected on the east range of what is to be the new quadrangle. The roofs are yet open to the sky – a kind of modern ruin! In return for my patronage of its completion, I am to be listed among the University benefactors, and to receive preference of attention whenever I visit in future. Paterson promised certain advantages for my sons, should those theoretical beings wish to attend Edinburgh for college.

Edinburgh distinguishes itself with its serious work on the sciences – especially the medical – which some English university men might call radical. My Cambridge education was weighted down with the Classics and Theology, and I prefer the philosophy of these radical institutions that pursue practical knowledge. One needs a bit of each. Perhaps the medical men can make some progress on surgery for the horrible cancer of the breast that carried away mother, that future mothers and sons may be spared. Our old English schools are too conservative, too pleased with themselves, too rich already.

Paterson is remarkably skilled in social lubrication without becoming a tiresome toady. I quite admire the Scots. They are a brusque, efficient, and serious set, but they let their hair down beneath the wigs in good company.

His friend MacDonnell sang out a Burns verse after dinner:

> The warly race may riches chase

An' riches still may fly them, O,
An' tho at last they catch them fast,
Their hearts can ne'er enjoy them, O.

But gie me a canny hour at e'en,
My arms about my dearie, O,
An' warly cares and warly men
May a' gae tapsalteerie, O!

Might I disclaim my worldly self to encircle my dearie, O! I am
served up as a spit-roasted pig to the busy and topsy-turvy world.
I was put in mind of another verse by the Scottish bard that
delighted me as a child, his poem to the Mouse, which perfectly
encompasses my present situation:

The best-laid schemes o' mice and men
    Go oft awry,
And leave us naught but grief and pain,
    For promised joy!
Still thou art blessed compared with me,
The present only toucheth thee:
But, Och! I backward cast my e'e
    On prospects drear!
And forward, tho' I cannot see,
    I guess an' fear!

As a boy I was that mouse, touched only by the light of present
concerns. Now I am the man haunted by regret of misconduct,
and cowed by visions of an unpromising future without my love.
Howl, howl, howl. My self-pity grows absurd, unmanly,
farcical. Onwards!

Georgie and Mrs. Annesley are beguiled by Edinburgh, and my
sister persuaded me to invest in a gentle Jennet at auction in the
square. The seller claimed her to be but two years of age, and
indeed her teeth are bright and sound. I made a bargain of two

and thirty guineas for the well-muscled beast, so my sister will have a trustworthy mare to bear her around Pemberley's trails.

30 June   Pemberley

We have returned safely home, Georgie riding side-saddle half the way on her mare, myself riding other times to exercise my limbs, and Mrs. Annesley holding down the carriage throughout. The season is full open, and a beautiful one it has become! I am almost recovered from my depression of spirits, though I constantly make reference to my new philosophy of easy discourse, open manners, and non-judgment. I talked as readily with doctor, professor, innkeeper, and street vendor in Edinburgh, and found them each agreeable in their distinct ways. Rather than shut myself up in the prison-house of my own thoughts, my manners are emancipated.

Might EB see the new me! How could I arrange an encounter? Would I dare to present myself to her unbidden? Has my letter, gruff as it was, changed her opinion?

In my absence a letter from Bingley came, in the company of a heavy parcel. He invites me to Dawlish, where his family will be enjoying a seaside vacation beginning tomorrow se'en-night. He says he may only accept my invitation to Pemberley if I accept his own hospitality. The letter was jovial; shades of the old happy Bingley. In the parcel was a large naval bar-shot of the type Denny recommended for muscular development. Bingley attached a name on a string: The Task-master.

I might ride Heeler hard to Dawlish in four days, once I complete some business in Lambton and write my letters. I might leave by the day after tomorrow. I would charge round the world had I an iron horse that never tired. Heeler is the nearest thing, until we invent the moving steam-engine.

4 July   On my roads in Oxfordshire

Last evening I was accosted by the saddest husk of a highway
man I ever beheld. He rode an ass, and pointed an ancient pistol,
riddled with rust, in the general direction of my heart as he
bumped bop bop bop up the road in my path. "A do-nashon
iffen ya phleeze, mah-sta!" He flicked the barrel towards his
outstretched palm. I dug my heels in Heeler's flanks and my
stout palfrey charged ahead, lowering his head to bump the
helpless blackguard from his jenny. Down went our challenger
in a heap of blubber and dust. His pistol flew off into the bush.
His whaling tears aroused my pity, and, rather than turning over
my whole purse, I placed a shining shilling on his upturned lapel,
and wished him a good evening of the local swill.

To-day is America's twenty-first birthday. I have stopped at the
University, somewhat out of my way, to make some
comparisons between the Tory mode of Oxford and the Whigs in
Edinburgh. Not a single mortar-boarded black robed-whelp in
Oxford made a whisper of the American anniversary – their
noses are glued in old books of philosophy and sermons. I was
so recently one of them – though wearing the fairer blue than
Oxford's royal. I raised a pint to our adolescent offspring,
America, within the hearing of the swillers, and received a
mixture of contemptuous and baleful looks in return. The bar-
man and I spoke of sailor insurrections on the South coast, as the
beach at Dawlish is my destination. His son a seaman at
Portsmouth was put in the stocks for a full day last April and
received fifteen lashes for his part in the protests of unlivable
wages. The ale-man is yet livid at the insult, and swears the
kingdom will fail if she treats her men-at-arms like enslaved
labour. He made not the link to our King's dealings with the
American Colonies some quarter of a century ago.

I am fortunate to have arrived on a regatta day, and the Thames is thick with sculls, shouts and carousing. The races continue to-morrow, so I have secured a bed at the inn for the next two nights, and shall sit in the shade bank-side and feed the swans as I watch the lads straining at their sculls. I am chary of Dawlish before the Bingleys are there to soften its hell-bent delights, and it is pleasant to be alone among the wildflowers on the bank-side of the Thames, with Heeler cropping the mead at my side.

7 July   Pleasant Row, Dawlish

With his brother's ample legacy, Frank Bingley has bought a new house by the sea-side, and I am his most esteemed and gentle guest, tho' estimable and gentle only to those outside my skin. Within, I still have my moments of feeling the rogue and peasant slave. Uncle Bingley is recoiling from business for a precious few weeks, and has assembled his new family about him – Charles, Caroline, Louisa, Hurst, the three youngest daughters, his companion Mrs. Bingley, and their personal servants. I am an honourary member of the family. Caroline is full of questions about Georgie, Pemberley, our recent travels, my horse, my tailor, my barber, my haberdasher, my health. She says she sees such a glow about me as to doubt whether I'm in love, insane, or in the last throes of consumption. It is as if nothing ever passed between us last winter, excepting that by the example of EB, she has strategically grown cheeky with me.

Uncle Bingley, *monsieur bourgeois*, asked me to stroll about town in the evening, filled with a desire to speak with a man of consequence. Dawlish is rapidly growing into a fashionable watering-hole, and each week old fields are plowed into new sandy rows, then forthwith paved with cobbles and screwed with leisure houses. Bingley hopes his early purchase on Pleasant Row will appreciate as word gets to the elite of Manchester and Birmingham regaling the pleasures of the warm South.

He complimented my effect on his nephew, who is as serious and studious as ever he saw Charles. I accepted credit where I should have endured censure, since my friend's newfound devotion to business is a consequence of his aching heart, a matter on my head. Frank Bingley has heard Charles's objections to the slave labour in the West Indies, and plans to pull out of his involvements there and transplant completely over to tea in the East Indies and China, tho' the returns are less certain. This, I knew already through Charles.

The landed gentry, said he, have little cause to bother with matters beyond our own borders, as their wealth, capital, and labour are likewise domestic. He claims to have weightier and more complex business concerns to balance, in addition to adopting his brother's five daughters, four of whom remain unmarried, and a sister-in-law accustomed to the finest delicacies and fashions. "Let them eat cake" has become one of her standby twittering jokes with her daughters, when any person of lesser wealth complains of their penury. Bingley's brother let his family become dissipated, indulgent, and silly, whilst he was off labouring to pay their bills. It is pitiful to descend from such heights – so his only solution is to marry them advantageously.

I thought this speech would end with Caroline leaping from the nearest alley, wrapped in nothing but a ribbon. Instead, the cracked old jade winked at me and said: I'm proud to have a newfangled house in leisure-land; I'm proud of the Bingley fortune wrought by my and my brother's sweat and wits; I'm proud that my nephew is a well-liked and comely young man. All I wish is for my family to be respected and loved by the likes of you, my gentle young man, and your presence here makes me proud of them. We must have done *something* right, to be favoured by the presence of a Darcy on holiday, eh? He clapped my back and chuckled all the way back to Pleasant Row.

The men plan a ride up to Exeter Cathedral tomorrow morning.

7 July   Exeter Cathedral

Hurst and Uncle Bingley nearly perished in the heat, but at last their girth was borne uphill by solid horseflesh to Exeter, where we spent a pleasant day poking around the grounds of the venerable pile. We measured the longest vaulted ceiling in England, we strained to hear the tock of the astronomical clock, we weighed our knees against the misericords, and made purchase of several post-cards imprinted with the edifice, which Bingley and I will send to the four kingdoms at Pemberley, Grosvenor, Netherfield, and Dawlish. We are tourists, fully at the mercy of the local bauble bursars and purveyors in watered ales, and we have spent our pennies liberally.

Hurst and his horse spent most of the day in the shade of a great oak on the cathedral lawn, the first examining his hip-flask and then his inner eye-lids, and the second shearing all the soft turf within his rein-length. Uncle Bingley, quite indifferent to the divine since God deals not in shillings, soon turned to beating on all the local trade doors in hopes of extending his tea business to the South-west coast of England.

These gentlemen dispatched to their noble pursuits, Charles and I have been free to talk all afternoon. Bingley is somewhat recovered from the winter disappointments, he smiles and praises every new prospect, he spoke glowingly of a secret gift of five hundred pounds he made to Mayor's wife (the dead soldier in the West Indies). Despite his munificence, I suspect that his most genuine recovery will be to return to Netherfield again. He wants to see Miss Bennet, "however little she cares for me," when hunting season returns. I wished him joy with the mission, and gainsaid his invitation so as to gain time to think. I was on the very edge of confessing the whole history of

Netherfield and Longbourn; it nearly came tumbling from my soul like a fervent prayer at the altar.

I held my tongue, however. I would like to see Jane Bennet again myself, and study her countenance in Bingley's company, before I blather a self-condemning confession. To take her sister's word as the final truth of the matter is a species of surrender.

But how would I study one, without crossing the path of the other?

10 July   Pleasant Row, Dawlish

I could grow fat as a whale spouting port wine by the wine-dark seas were I to tarry in Dawlish any longer. My swimming shirt is soaked with brine, my skin turns brown, I dine on oysters delivered live by wandering fishermen, and I have grown inattentive to everything but the drift of the sun in the summer sky. The most indulgent vacationers idle here, and they cut an amusing figure, preening and prancing about, showing ancles and low bodices, dragging expensive laces through the sand.

Segregation of the sexes is entirely ignored. I am whispered to be in courtship with at least a half dozen of the local beauties, and Bingley is responsible for the rest. Neither of us has lifted a finger to deserve such attention, but I am in good humour. One lady, a sultry suss named Miss Buttersby, of Leeds, left open the bathing-machine to my full view as she changed from her swimming frock, and, *entre nous*, I glimpsed somewhat higher than her ancles, and lower than her bodice. Scandalously, deliciously improper! She is a tradesman's daughter. Shall I become a satyr? My conscience commands me to avoid such easy temptations. I would not abuse the whole of the opposite sex as a punishment for my frustrated desire for one woman.

I must return to the world.

12 July   Grosvenor Square

I assuaged the Bingleys in my departure only by extending my invitation beyond Charles to his eldest two sisters as well. They will all join me at Pemberley in the course of a few weeks, should they crawl out of Dawlish before drowning in high tide. Georgie will come to-morrow to London to meet with a new piano tutor. I shall give her free range of Lamb's Conduit Street to select a modern wardrobe with Empire waist-lines, and I mean to take her to browse through a collection of fine India muslins at the Middleton and Innes warehouse on Chancery Lane, which are advertised as some of the finest ever to reach our shore via the East India Company.

Thanks be to the whims of fashion that ladies are free to exercise and draw natural breath than ever they were before in this century. I recall as a young boy sitting outside my mother's room on the night of the annual Darcy Soirée, how her *femme de chambre* tugged and strained against her vile corsets to recover an eighteen inch waist two months after Georgie's birth. What cries of agony, sweat, and tears rattled that door, and what a dusted pile of flounce appeared in the place of my mother! I was relieved to recover the gentle, mild, pink person in a simple gown, who appeared the day after our guests had gone.

I have not told Georgie as yet, but I wish for her to consider whether she will come out in next year's season, liberated from wigs, hoops, and lead powder. Perhaps strolling around the streets on my arm will give her the courage to attend stifling balls and endure officious youths. I must assist her in repelling avaricious eyes, to find a man who truly loves her for who she is. Yet she presents so little of herself to the public eye, I wonder how a young man would ever gain her confidence? It is through my confidence in her that she may emerge from her girlish shell.

We are both of us hobbled in society and misunderstood for our shyness.

14 July   Grosvenor Square

To-day is the eight year anniversary of the fall of the Bastille. It was stolidly ignored in London.

18 July   Marylebone Park, London

What changes mark the seasons since last I walked in Marylebone Park! It was the darkest afternoon in December; now, walking with Georgie, it is a fusion of electric green, dappled shade, and sheep-flock clouds. We have settled in the shade of a hedge-row for lunch; Georgie sketches the passing scenes, and here I write.

What has occurred? I sent off my spy Bloom to the neighborhood of Meryton, and he returned yesterday with a few points of interest. First, the militia are gone from the village, and Wickham with them. That makes my return there more favourable. Next, only three of the Bennet sisters are to be found at Longbourn, though Bloom could not discern which ones are abroad. He did not risk speaking directly to Mrs. Phillips again, who would now know that he is not a new recruit, so he spoke with a yeoman riding his jenny into the village. He is a tenant of the small Bennet estate. The yeoman was only partly acquainted with the affairs at the mansion-house, the demands of his farm is adequate excuse for this limited intelligence.

This Mr. Wragg believed one of the younger Bennet daughters has left for Brighton with the Colonel's wife and the militia; and one of the elder daughters just left on a travelling vacation with her aunt and uncle from London – whither, he was unsure, but he believed their destination to be the Lakes. Presumably this is the same London tradesman, the uncle named Gardiner, as Jane Bennet was visiting last winter.

Bloom did not wish to rouse his suspicion with further interrogation, so they spoke of the season and his luck for the past few years of farming. It seems that Mr. Bennet is a pleasant, if somewhat neglectful, landlord. When directly appealed for favours – improvements to the buildings, equipment, small loans – he is willing to provide, but those tenants reluctant to ask directly for assistance are not likely to see him emerge from his own house. He has not a head for agriculture, so they must live by their own talents and wits.

Bennet's neglect is not like Aunt Catherine's – it is the neglect of a man who finds more pleasure in books than in dirt – a man who does not like to give or receive trouble from anyone. My Aunt seeks out what trouble she can cause and labels it perspicacity. Wragg expressed satisfaction with his situation on the Bennet lands, where he may freely make choices that benefit his family without cheating his master, and he is not driven into the ground by an overzealous overseer such as my Aunt. Bennet has no ambitions to appear better than his subordinates. He is merely shy, and wants not the trouble of frequent interaction. That mode I know well.

Wragg reported on Mrs. Bennet's bitter disappointment with recent lost prospects of her two eldest daughters. My shadow lingers there still. Wragg and the other tenants are unsettled by the prospect of the entailment, which would cast them over to a new owner of uncertain character. Wragg was not impressed with the village chatter about Mr. Collins, when he visited. Though some ladies labeled him agreeably talkative, loyal, and large, Wragg heard first-hand from his master that Collins was a fatuous dunce, whose primary value was as a study in muttonheadedness. Wragg wishes that his master might live to a wizened old age.

Is it She traveling to the Lakes? Is she framing the same scenes as Georgie and I so recently did? What are her thoughts on the picturesque and poetry? Have our roads crossed with the separation of only a few weeks?

Might I hazard sharing my torment with my sister? I told her yesterday of EB's piano playing, and how artless and easy her air. I dared no further.

Well, well. Georgie has completed her sketch. It is a misty, symmetrical prospect of hedges, fountains, and floating parasols. Her eye is abstract and subjective – quite unlike our realist portraiture of the day. Were she to sketch me I would appear a tanned rhombus with a coiffe of brown bubbles.

Onwards back to Grosvenor.

26 July   Grosvenor Square

Gibson last week sent me a letter, which I just received today, requesting my attention in the business of the Demussy tract. The family is eager to sell now that old Demussy is six feet below, and liquidate their land in preference for the London life. They have accepted my low bid for their farms – some five hundred acres of varied land and fifteen hearty and longstanding tenants, all in the general neighborhood of my own estate – because of the recent poor harvests and desperation of the family to raise ready cash. I will attend this opportunity with Gibson and the Demussy steward, Everdon, before other eager purchasers emerge, and before my guests arrive to Pemberley in a few days' time. Thus I hasten away to-morrow morning and hope to arrive by the following evening. The party, Georgie and the Bingleys, are expected by Mrs. Reynolds on 30 July if their roads are clear.

27 July   Lamplighter's Inn, Aylesbury

Heeler threw a shoe on the cobbles just as I was leaving town. As they say, "no horse, no shoe," so I was obliged to stop off within the city limits. I was already later than planned, having paid my respects to Johnson in his St. Paul's shop. I had acquired a volume of Priestley's theories of air and phlogiston, and a new volume of poems by Southey, which Johnson said he could recommend in praise of the poet's ideas, and regret for the censurable defects of the verse.

These safely in my saddle-bag, upon losing one shoe of four ahead of a long journey, I stopped off at a livery-stable in Moorfields called the Swan and Hoop just by the Finsbury Circus. This mischance, and a detour from the Sparrow's Herne Turnpike made necessary to avoid a drover and his immense flock near Boxmore, delayed my arrival at Derbyshire by a day. I am laid over for the night, and shall not arrive at Pemberley until the morning of the 29th. Heeler, a gallant palfrey, can average fifty miles a day for a week on end, if I require it of him. He shall have his rest in his accustomed stables at home.

It was pleasant to spend an hour in wait for my new horse shoe, as it was a reason to associate with East-enders again. With a long ride ahead I did not stop off in a pub, but kept to the stable yards and observed the busy efficiency of the keeper and his men. I was amused by the ostler's young sons, John and George, who reminded me of younger British versions of Henri and Remy. John is a vigorous child of about two years, with rich brown hair and dark hazel eyes, quite steady on his legs for one so young and jealously protective of his infant brother George, who he held close in his arms as he proudly presented him to the visiting stranger. These working-class children grow up fast, with no-one to fuss over them, and I expect George was as secure with his brother as any child with a grown nurse. After thinking a minute, little John spoke to me slowly in rhymes:

> the gentle man
> from the west en'
> must surely spen'
> his pennies blan'
> in father's han'
> then make his way
> tho' he may stay
> from dawn to day
> but make his way
> to the green lan'
> to the green quiet lan'…

His mind seemed far away as he repeated the last line. I doubt little John has ever been out of London, though his imagination strays far from his father's stables on the East end. I returned his verse with a few lines from my new volume of Southey, a tale of a wandering urchin:

> With wayward feet a pilgrim woe begone,
> Life's upward road I journeyed many a day,
> And hymning many a sad yet soothing lay,
> Beguil'd my wandering with the charms of song.
> Lonely was my heart and rugged was my way,
> Yet often pluck'd I as I passed along,
> The wild and simple flowers of Poesy,
> etc. etc.

The child was delighted with the folk rhyme, and begged me to read a string of sonnets. We passed from plucking poesy's flowers to Southey's laments on the perils of the sable race, and little John questioned me closely with a series of piping little inquisitions, "whut's a sabul rice?" Southey sermonized about the "sable race worn with toil" and the "pale tyrant" who rules o'er. Sweetening with maple sugar, rather than cane from the hot colonies, is Southey's solution to our guilt. We had a running conversation, the father Thomas at his farrier's work, his son John parsing out my story, and infant George cooing in full pleasure of fine day. Thomas says the elder boy's been gabbing fanatically since he was six months old – and now is in a phase of speaking in improvised rhymes. I paid father Thomas not with "pennies bland" but with a shining sovereign, and left John's hand full of pennies that I bid him dedicate to maple syrup. My heart was well-full with the child's company as Heeler trotted me up the North road.

Tomorrow I shall leave early and ride hard, with the long day to my advantage. I plan to stop to-morrow night in Leicester.

29 July   Pemberley

Grace. Hope. She came to me! I saw and spoke to her this very day. I touched her arm and looked into her eyes. I hardly know what I said at first. She was wearing a travelling dress, had tanned skin and a look of wondrous agitation. We shared that space of pain and pleasure, pleasurable pain, until called back to the mere world where we live in separate bodies. She came to me today! Rather I came to her, for she and her friends were strolling across the front green as I emerged from the stables, quite exercised from the two-day's ride. Not in the Lakes, but on my own lawn, by my own lake! With what restraint did I half-contain the delight rushing in. At that moment of surprise the tight bolus within my ribs – the seat of my soul – relaxed, and an electric fire rushed to my limbs.

Which gods might I thank for this second chance? Which forces of fate aligned to draw her back into my fold? Surely this is a cosmic reward for my renovation. Or is this blessed day less spiritual, and more practical, than I have allowed? Perhaps she came to my estate to reconsider me, to see what kind of man I am by the home I keep. Indeed, the home is a symbol of the man, and if my lady likes wandering watery woodsy walks, as they are mine, they are hers. If she desires loyal and intelligent servants, they will provide for her comfort. Did she imagine today that it might be something to be mistress at Pemberley? My home is not elaborate like Rosings, but she must have noted the sound architecture, the long vistas, the varied landscape, the coves and cloisters. Were our youth infinite, I would show her every blade of grass.

She promised to come tomorrow again. The paths wear the sweep of her skirts. I can hardly hold my pen still for the heat in my soul. I am sure she does not hate me. I saw her embarrassment, her confusion, I spoke gently and she responded, turned towards me, saw *me* and not the stern man who oft inhabits my face. She was not saucy or defiant. She was immersed with me. She approved of Pemberley. I shall bring her closer. I long to acquaint her with my sister who comes tomorrow. I shall find true happiness for the first time. Heavens! She lies five miles away tonight.

30 July   Pemberley

We have had the happiest day I can recall, excepting yesterday. Georgie and the Bingleys arrived and I took my sister and Charles without delay to the inn in Lambton where Elizabeth and her relatives, the Gardiners of London are staying. Though Georgie is shy, I felt the affinity between the women who value talent and exertion rather than its appearance. All my hopes for my sister have already been embodied in Elizabeth. I saw the blush rush to her cheeks and we held one another's gaze levelly, plumbing the depths of our dark and complex history without need of words. With Bingley she exchanged a warm regard and memory of our times at Netherfield. Bingley hinted around his curiosity about her sister, and I believe we both found his continued interest in Jane pleasing.

The party spent half an hour discussing divers topics, traveling, fishing, trade, and the fine season, each one of us rooting out the thoughts of the others, and in a spirit of open jollity as has no equal in my recollection. At last, there was no one present to cloud the pure joy of the assembly. I was as open and true to my affections as decorum allowed, which means I was quite overflowing with love for Elizabeth, and respect for her relations. The Gardiners are intelligent, energetic people – fully superior in manner to some of my own celebrated relations. I wish to know them better.

We have arranged for the travelling party to join us at Pemberley tomorrow, where we may join the other Bingleys in a small reunion of friends and enemies. It cannot be avoided that Caroline and Louisa will be there, but I am not afraid. Elizabeth will have the full protection of my regard. I believe she already feels it. I have dismissed my emotional guards and sent them packing to the devil. I have engaged Gardiner for some fishing, where I may further acquaint myself with his talents and business. There after I will dedicate myself to his niece.

I took no wine with dinner – I need no intoxication beyond her presence. Come, tomorrow!

I spent the late afternoon in Lambton with Gibson and Everdon, closing on the Demussey tract. That acquisition is momentous indeed – it increases my landholdings in Derbyshire by a full third. Gibson is running in circles in anticipation of the increase in tenants and rents, and fortunately he is a man who flourishes under a heavy load of work. Yet this acquisition pales in comparison to the return of my love! Smithson in London will receive the packet that closes all final business, and I shall devote no further mind to it at present. My brain is ravished.

31 July   Pemberley

Morning came early and Bingley, Hurst, Gardiner, and myself
spent several hours fishing. Hurst returned to the house two
hours before luncheon, growling of his privations and the
idleness of angling, and he left us to pursue more torpid idleness
indoors. We were rather more at ease the three of us at the river
in peace. Gardiner is quite deft at the rod for a city man, and
regaled us with droll tales of fishes weighing a stone he'd
hooked on the Thames north of London – until I caught him
winking. Bingley succeeded in drawing him out more about his
elder nieces, and Charles basked in Gardiner's praises of Jane's
good humour, modesty, and beauty. Gardiner hopes to model
his own two daughters after Jane and Elizabeth, and his wife
recruits them as often as can be spared from Longbourn to spend
time with their cousins. After we caught a good sized carp each,
and Gardiner a pike as well, my impatience to see Elizabeth
overwhelmed everything else, and we hastened back to change
into proper clothes.

I wished to relieve her from Caroline's inquisitions, and indeed
Caroline had drawn her sword by the time we entered the room.
Caroline soon alluded to the rakish redcoats in Meryton, and
jabbed at Elizabeth about her sisters' flirtations. The whole
party were mortified in suspense of such ill treatment of one
guest by another, my sister especially, until Elizabeth replied
only, young ladies, Miss Bingley, must be excused if they form
silly designs upon impossible men, for their education has given
no better example. Caroline meant to rejoin with a more specific
harangue, but her brother leaped into the conversation with a
sudden rapture on Spanish blood oranges, and presented
Caroline with a plate of sliced hothouse nectarines to fill her
mouth.

After this moment, I scarce removed my gaze from Elizabeth through the course of the evening. I see no reason to conceal my love from anyone any longer. She met my eyes with such a steady regard as to support my hopes for our future. We had thirty seconds by the carriage when I took her pelisse from Sutton and dismissed him. Her aunt and uncle had wandered again to the front stream in talk of fishing. I asked for the honour of attending her in the morning, which she approved with a coy smile. Her embarrassment has not yet ceased, and she apologized again for forcing her company on the Pemberley party. I enjoined that there could be no sweeter enforcement of a friendship than hers, and that I had learned a scholar's stack of wisdom in the few passing weeks of our total acquaintance. Her eyes rose to mine, and she said (I shall never forget her words) Then, sir, you have spent a good deal too much time as a whining school-boy, and a good deal too little as a sighing lover. You know the seven ages? Perhaps we have shifted into the next one together. She presented me with her hand to assist her into the carriage. Instead I lifted it to my lips. After a moment her relations returned, and I was forced to bid her adieu.

My open affection did not, as I had hoped, check Caroline's insults after our guests had left, so I told her directly that Elizabeth was the very embodiment of beauty. I also reminded her that as the sister of my friend, she was a guest in my house and would behave with the gentleness expected of one. She said not another word all night, and Bingley's look of bemusement showed this retort was a long time overdue.

After everyone had gone to bed, I walked the paths again in the darkness for several miles, living the day over by the light of the moon, my brain lit with visions of her. I skipped along the river like a lad of twelve, as I used to do under the leafing chestnuts and wandering stars. Back then I dreamed of pagan fairies in the deep woods, their slender forms slipping behind cedars and birches just as I glanced at them. Now I am so near the fleshly form of joy, my living fairy shall not elude me.

I shall hasten to Lambton after breakfast tomorrow and pursue my suit.

I have never felt more awake with delight – and now I must try to sleep through the night!

3 August   Grosvenor Square

Great changes have come. Wickham's vicious propensities have emerged with a vengeance. His behaviour, never properly directed by my counsel as it ought to have been, is endangering everything. Elizabeth's tears are hardly dry on my sleeve. What torment – my ardent journey to Lambton with a design to renew my addresses became a sad scene of consolation in her moment of distress, and I left with my resolve to assist her family undeclared. But alas I could promise her nothing until I succeed in my new mission. My hand is forced. What powers I have are devoted to restoring the Bennets to respectability, and placing W in a situation where he may live securely.

I am in London attempting to locate the rogue, who has absconded with none other than Lydia Bennet, Elizabeth's youngest and wildest sister. They are thought to have eloped, though I cannot believe Wickham intends to marry Lydia without some financial relief. His debts are extreme. Gibson is fully on the case, trying to locate Mrs. Younge, and I expect Gardiner to meet with me tomorrow, after he has left Elizabeth in Hertfordshire with her miserable family.

Somehow, W surmised my affection for Elizabeth, and means to ruin her through her sister. Is it possible? Am I afflicted with *paranoea*? He conversed with her many times, both before and after our understanding emerged at Rosings. Perhaps she spoke to him about her new knowledge of his behaviour, and he deduced that only my regard for her would explain this intelligence? Could Fitzwm have scolded W for his slanders on my character?

It cannot be a pure coincidence that W would abscond with Elizabeth's sister, thus ruining the prospects of all Bennets. Though it re-asserts my ego to place my fortunes at the center of his machinations, I cannot believe this to be a random act. W's appearances in my life are design or destiny, not chance. If I am to live the life I chuse, I must settle him once and for all. My mind was in a tumult the whole journey southwards – and now I am in a position to act.

If I may not tame W with scolding, I will squelch him with generosity. I have all the powers of my cheque book to make him a proper husband of Lydia. He is the kind of man who is easily bought, though the expenditure may be dear. Elizabeth is my only object, and to think of her in relation to mere money is laughable. Yes, I shall part with a cold quid in exchange for hot happiness. But I must make it out so she never knows.

It is only eight in the evening. I shall go out again to the streets to seek W so we may begin the settlement.

7 Aug   Grosvenor Square

I dared not write until I had some certain information of the lost couple, and some hope that I had power to resolve our common distress. It is Monday and I have been all morning in the company of Mrs. Younge, who now keeps a lodging house in Edward Street. Smithson gets credit for locating her, for he used his old contacts at Gray's Inn to scare up intelligence of a landlady whose boarders are often in need of legal representation. Once Gibson passed on to me Mrs. Younge's location, I hastened directly to her parlor with all the force of our former history behind my resolve.

I have not yet seen the couple, but after several hours of interrogation, and thirty quid besides, Mrs. Younge's lips loosened. She says they are boarded in a small apartment in the Old Kent Road, living in seclusion. Wickham has been plying Mrs. Younge for resources since they arrived in London some ten days ago – the very same time I was blissful at Pemberley! As he has no money, she has arranged for the couple's lodging until Wickham can decide on his next move. I suspect that Mrs. Younge only betrayed W's location because she sees money in it, for herself and for W. She sneered at my clothes, my carriage, my bribes, until I had named her price.

It is near midnight, and I am exhausted and jittery. I must wait 'till morn to call at the Old Kent Road.

8 Aug   Grosvenor Square

They are discovered. W was cloudy after an evening of heavy drink and dissipation, but his morning fog lifted fast when he saw my face. Lydia Bennet seems confused about their circumstances, and mangy in appearance, but she is still credulous to whatever story W tells her. She believes he is making wedding arrangements, and that I am an old friend. By my oath, her understanding is no longer far from the truth!

Immediately on their discovery I sent Gibson, who had come with me, to call on the Gardeners in Gracechurch Street, and bring them in haste. I would not leave W once I had found him. Within the hour both Mr. and Mrs. Gardiner arrived, and Mrs. Gardiner removed Lydia in the pretense of taking fresh air and shopping, so that W, Gardiner, and myself could begin to settle the business.

W is more broken and less haughty than I had expected. He is under severe distress of his creditors – a string of them from Lambton to Meryton to Brighton to London – and he seemed truly frightened that he was soon to be carried off to Fleet Prison. His concealment was falling away after more than a week in hiding, and harassing collectors were calling at his door. When he saw my face, he welcomed a friend in me – thus the depth of his circumstances!

It is far better to treat him as a friend than as my sworn enemy. It accords with my own reformation over the past months, and if the man is ever to be my brother-in-law, I should rather have a hand in restoring him to respectability than cast him out to the wolves. He is my symbolic brother of old. He plaintively reminded me of our fine times in Pemberley woods. I would before have seen this gesture as petty manipulation, but my heart is larger now. Gardiner, more acutely concerned for his niece, had less patience with his nostalgia, and I had to interfere before the man boxed W's ears.

All that we could accomplish today was to remove the couple from Old Kent Road to my spare rooms in Grosvenor Square, where I may have complete control over their movements, and where they may exist in relative secresy from W's creditors. Sutton and Bloom are completely discreet. W spent the afternoon drawing up a list of the names of those to whom he is in debt, and Gibson is burning the midnight oil writing letters requesting invoices.

Lydia, for her part, has been accommodated with ablutions, a new dress, and a quiet evening by the fireside with my library and pianoforte at her disposal. She is well-behaved, or in a state of awe, perhaps, but thus far has made no trouble. She spoke but little at dinner, her aunt and uncle and myself adding considerable severity to the company of Wickham. She did emit a series of ejaculations by way of thanks: Lord! What a fat pig! … Lord! How rich you are Mr. Darcy! … By God I was weary of that nasty hole at Old Kent! … Are we to see Covent Garden theatre tomorrow? …My aunt only took me to the dirty shops in the East end. …How I long to shop on Bond Street! … I've never tasted such smacking wine, all the way from Italy!

Though she reminds me but little of her elder sisters, I take pleasure in entertaining any Bennet.

10 Aug   Grosvenor Square

Gibson sent the letters to W's creditors by express two days ago, and we await the final tally. Wickham has estimated in the range of ten thousand pounds, and I have prepared Gibson to discharge a sum in that amount once we can secure it, and for Smithson to oversee the documents. In the meantime, we wait.

The Gardiners have written to Longbourn with news of the couple's discovery. How I longed to send the letter myself, or to *be* the letter, post-haste at their door, to witness Elizabeth's countenance! As we have no particulars yet to relate, G said to Mr. Bennet only that they are found and that he will sort out the financial and nuptial arrangements. Mrs. G takes charge of her niece every day in the morning, and returns with her not before supper, so as to give us some peace in the meantime.

Fitzwilliam came to-day, in the dual interest of helping me, and interrogating Wickham. We had an animated talk this afternoon, the three of us. Indeed, Fitzwm wrote to W in Meryton after our time at Rosings, scolding him for spreading untruths about me to strangers, and in his letter he mentioned my blackened reputation in Elizabeth's eyes. In his zeal to defend me and my broken heart, but he appears to have let in the viper of W's revenge. W is a man too canny to opportunity to pass by such a dainty one, and he concluded rightly that Fitzwm would not have mentioned

EB in particular, had not her opinion been weighty to myself. Once he found in Lydia a credulous and silly girl, loose from her family in Brighton, he made his move. He claims not to have thought through the pursuit of his creditors once his position with the militia was lost. I was still the sole target of his revenge!

Seen in a charitable light, it is a credit to his regard for Georgie that his severe disappointment would drive him to such extremes of revenge. Though he is thoughtless and selfish when it comes to the far-ranging consequences of his actions, I, too, am not above similar censure for my selfishness, and the consequences I have felt for my earlier neglect of his living. Wickham and Bingley are both victims of my past self-absorption, and I will forbear and make it all right.

Fitzwm is working on finding W a commission in some remote soldiery, perhaps where he has contacts in Newcastle. W, for his part, has promised to marry Lydia once I have dealt with his debts. We hope to have Mr. Bennet agree to settle some small annuity on her as a dowry, to help them maintain a household once they are settled.

I left F and W in the library to discuss the particulars of his possible commission, and I have retired to bed. That spot between my ribs, the one I call my soul, is easier now.

All's well that ends well – if I be relieved of no more than ten thousand pounds, I will return to abject giddiness! And my I now escape to dreams of her.

12 Aug   Grosvenor Square

I received many letters today – the last of the credit reports, an admonition from my Aunt, who seems also to have sniffed out my passion for EB, and a letter of concern from Bingley, who has arrived in London but will remain at Russell Square until I welcome a visit. I am a bad liar, and I gave him little explanation of my flight from Pemberley. Least expected of all, to my door came a letter from Justine, postmarked last month from Calais.

The grand total to buy the groom: £8,366

I will make it a clear £8,500 to dispatch the wedding expenses and the couple's transport thereafter to Hertfordshire.

Gardiner has notified his brother-in-law of Lydia's joy, and the wedding is set for three days hence. Bennet has promised £100 a year for his youngest daughter, though the father's confusion about how so little a sum could settle the business was inked all over his reply. He shall have to remain in ignorance, and trust that cosmic good fortune has fallen in his lap.

I have allayed Bingley by writing to beg that we might return to Netherfield for some hunting in the course of a few weeks – but that urgent business etc. etc. presently occupies me.

My sainted Aunt Catherine. Ah. How has she been informed? What explanation do I owe her? I cannot speak publicly of my regard until its return is assured to me from Elizabeth's lips. My Aunt shall have to thrash about in half-knowledge along with the rest of us.

Justine's letter was all energy. She and the whole family were on the eve of their departure for Philadelphia. Her father and brother, Julie, and the children, Sabine, Henri, and Remy, are *débordant d'entrain* – full of life -- and so conflicted with excitement for the future and nostalgia for their homeland that she could not properly sort one feeling from another. She assures me that *la famille du circumstance* is in complete harmony, and wishes me joy with my *amours Anglaises*. When they land and settle in America, I am promised to hear from her again.

With these points of business mostly settled, Fitzwm and I aim to enjoy ourselves to-night. We are off to my club for an evening of gentleman's whiskey and conversations. I am ignorant to everything that has passed in the wider world for the last fortnight. To-morrow, Sunday, is my day of rest.

17 Aug   Pemberley

I am returned to an empty mansion that echoes with birdsong from the open windows. I walk the hollow halls, stroll on the leaf-shaded paths, and tinker with the pianoforte keys so recently played. Everyone is elsewhere – I am alone with my thoughts and plans.

Mr. and Mrs. Wickham were quietly married and mailed off to their visit to Hertfordshire. Fitzwm arranged for W's commission at Newcastle to begin next week, as we both believed that a short stay with the couple would be adequate exposure for the Bennets.

Georgie and Mrs. Annesley left last week for Nottingham on a friendly visit, and are scheduled to remain there until next week. The Bingleys and Fitzwm are in London. Perhaps I should be there, too, tending to business, admiring new plays and fashions, discussing the great ideas of our age, lamenting the war and from armchairs planning the next battle.

But everything calls for calm, this moment. It is precious and rare. I must give her some space to bid adieu to her sister, before I arrive on the scene. Before Bingley arrives for Jane.

I spent half the afternoon on the front terrace leafing through an art book of Oriental sculpture. Abstract, clean, erotic, exotic. So falls Apollo from his long arc.

Mrs. Reynolds and Sutton, finished with their duties for the day, kept my company through dinner. We talked with jollity on the affairs of Pemberley estate and the fortunes of its farmers. I could see that Mrs. Reynolds was wild to inquire as to the lovely guest who so recently departed in haste. However, she held her station and talked determinedly of the state of the furniture, new and old, in the South wing. Her nephew is apprenticed to the cabinet maker in Derby, and wishes him to master to the art of restoration. I agreed to take him on for an extended commission, provided that I pay him apprentice rates.

Thereafter we discussed the fortunes of every family within a ten mile radius, but our conversation never alighted on the lady in my chest.

21 Aug   Pemberley

The early harvest has begun – the orchards are alive with boys and girls plucking apples, and the old men are cleaning their presses with vinegar and boiling water, in relish of cider-making.

I know not what to plan for, but in case I am more than usual distracted from my autumn duties this year, I have made early rounds to my farms and seen to their needs. Martin's boy broke his leg under a rickety wheel-barrow. I took Dr. Brigg's bill to set the bone, so that his father may concentrate on yields and preparing his harvest equipment. Our experiments with grasses are in full swing, and Sinclair attends to little else. He speaks of writing a report on the heterogeneous grazing sod this winter, in hopes it will find audience with the Royal Society. I shall lend my name to the document to provide secure patronage, and I have written to Dr. MacDonnell at Edinburgh to see whether some natural scientist on the faculty might review the work and introduce it to learned circles.

I spent yesterday afternoon closing the deal on the Demussy tract, which yet needs to be ratified by independent witness and approved by the local bailiff. The younger Demussys are in such debt that they must part with some portion of the land, and indeed they wish to dispatch with all of it so as to keep the estate intact, avoid further taxation, and devote their energies to trade and fashion in London. I hope to take charge of it early in 1798, and assign Gibson the major duties of its maintenance. The land is presently leased at 23 shillings an acre, which seems an oppressively high figure, and Gibson would like to relieve the tenants with lower rents for several years – down to 20 shillings.

Of the mansion house, Thrushmoor, and the ten acres of gardens surrounding, James Demussy is resolved to keep charge of it until some eligible purchase presents itself. I suggested that I might find him a buyer, though I did not mention Bingley by name. Bingley and Demussy were keen on the same young lady from Mayfair three seasons back, and I know not whether Demussy's more resentful temper would recall Bingley's superior graces of address and person. Since neither one married the girl, I cannot imagine the edge is still sharp. Of course I am ahead of myself: Bingley would have to *want* the mansion-house as his family estate, before his officious friend jumps in to acquire it.

At last. At last it is time to prepare for my journey to Hertfordshire. I promised to meet Bingley at Netherfield by the 26th – precisely nine months after his all-important ball. The servants are readying the house for our shooting party, and the Bingley sisters and Hurst have gone to Scarborough, thank God. We will be at peace to call on Longbourn trailed only by the local gossips.

My duties thus fulfilled here, I have dispatched a good-bye letter to my sister, who will return to Pemberley in three days, and stay as its mistress until Christmas.

My humour is to proceed at a lazy pace the hundred miles southwards to my heart.

25 Aug   Netherfield

'Twill be fresh poultry for dinner. It is a joy to spend a warm afternoon in the company of my dear friend, without the worry of business or society to distract us from our purposes here. We mean to hunt pheasant! And so we did. Charles and I each arrived a day before planned, giving us the leisure to walk for miles in circles around Netherfield, with one beater at the bushes ahead of us, and two hunters using their noses to find out nesting sites. After killing a half-dozen birds, our blood lust was quite exhausted, and we left our weapons and quarry with Bingley's serving man and proceeded peacefully on foot. Only then did I begin my confession.

With my best *mea culpa* attitude (which was after these months of revelation no put-on act), I rehearsed the history of my interference with Bingley's affections. He is aware of his sister's upward ambitions, and her pet project of uniting him with my sister, so it came as no surprise that she looked unfavourably on his alliance with Jane Bennet.

He was shocked to hear that I had supported Caroline's machinations, however. He trusted me to have spoken from true conviction of Jane's indifference, and so I thought I was speaking, at least partially. This volume documents my efforts at self-protection from her sister, which must have been my primary motivation. I could not confess that portion of the act to Bingley, so I left it with him that I regretted my interference and believed it to be based on a false apprehension of the lady's affections. I have the secret intelligence of Jane's true heart, from her sister's lips, so I felt confident in assuring him of Jane's ardent love just nine months after assuring him of her placid indifference.

Bingley is not a resentful fellow. His surprise melted away into delight, and such a ray of gladness spread over his face as dismissed any anger a less generous man might justly have held. After assuring him three times that I was now convinced that Jane had loved him very much, it was all I could do to delay him from leaping on his horse and clatter up to Longbourn. My caution won over there. We walked out the conversation back to Netherfield in preparation of his addresses to her, which he is determined to make as soon as he is sure of the renewal of their affection. He knew not whether to begin to speech with an apology or an avowal of his love. I know something by way of my own experience – begin a proposal with love, not regret.

I must go tomorrow too, acting at least as a rod in Bingley's spine as he faces the awful drawing-room of the Bennets. We will be relentlessly raked over by their eyes. Why do I feel sick with the idea of being in her presence? It is not sickly revulsion, no; it is the dizzy stomach of apprehension. Bingley is the lover tomorrow, not me. So near the goal, I will proceed with caution, and make sure that our ladies are predisposed to our proposals. I was so blinded by arrogance at Rosings, I made not sure of her heart before attempting to claim it. I shall be quiet and watchful, the conservative gentleman.

Just after I retired for bed, Howe knocked on my door, entered, and solemnly delivered me the large iron pan, compliments, he said, of the cook-maid. He asked me to inform him if I required any other tools from the scullery.

27 Aug   Netherfield Park

After an early church service populated by the local farmers, Bingley and I dressed with care and went on horseback to call on the Bennet family. I was feeling queasy shy, but screwed up my courage to meet with the formidable Mrs. Bennet and her daughters, all of whom we hoped would attend our arrival, excepting the youngest. To help with my nerve, I wore my new royal blue coat with fine white stripes and a gold cravat. I believe my routine of weight-lifting and fencing is showing in my more robust figure, and though I have no valet in my service at Netherfield, I made my toilet quite to my satisfaction.

Only the impassioned could be degraded to such abysses of vanity! Love has made a dandy of me.

Upon our arrival, the ladies were duly assembled in their small sitting room. I vowed to pay little heed to the burbles of Mrs. Bennet, so though I heard her allude to Lydia's marriage, to its shoddy advertisement, to the density of killable birds in the neighborhood, not one needle of it pierced the cushion of my propriety. I dedicated my attentions to the study of Jane Bennet, to see whether she was disposed to receive Bingley's attentions. I can say yea, upon this observation, and afterwards I said as much to him.

Of her sister, I know only that she was occupied with a small piece of needlework in the corner, and that whenever she seemed to be looking in my direction, I fixed my countenance on the assembly. It will not do to make puppy eyes across the room with a rabble of spies betwixt us. I am not paying visits as a lover, but as an escort to my friend Charles, whose affections have priority over mine. I did perceive, glancing once in her direction, that Elizabeth's complexion is glowing and her eyes lustrous. This fine image drove me back to the dedicated inspection of my polished boots. For all my seeming attention elsewhere, her singular presence obscures my sense of anything else.

This evening, Charles and I sipped brandy, feasted on pheasant, greens, and fresh cheese, and plotted out his every move for the next week. I shall attend a Bennet gathering in two days' time, upon his insistence, but soon after I must return to London to receive Gibson and Smithson's reports and divers news. Smithson writes that he has already received the parcel from the Pennsylvania frontier, and I am eager to scour the surveys.

After this first reunion, Bingley is as confident in Jane's affections as a man with no ego can fancy himself to be. I only assisted by lending him *my* ego, so he may believe himself worthy of her grace and beauty.

29 Aug   Netherfield Park

We have just returned from an evening party at the Bennet's. Just as I counted myself equal to conversation with her, I was quite damned by the seating gods all evening. I was perpetually surrounded by the least welcome company, and at the furthest range from Elizabeth. I exerted myself to engage pleasantly in conversation with everyone, even her mother, who was seated next to me at dinner. We managed to talk over the fashions of gentlemen in town in the heat of summer with relative concord. The conversation circled 'round loose fitting white linens and silken spun socks, and I informed her as to how the Directoire fashions had also affected male dress in recent years. She correctly supposed *my* attire to be custom tailored from the Bond Street shops, implying a kind of disapproval at my expenditure, though in the same breath she lamented her husband's thrift, his worn herringbone twill and dented tricome hat. I was secretly diverted by theories of how the matron's attitude towards my riches might change upon certain news, if ever I am to win the favour of her eldest daughter but one. How my ten thousand a year would ring the crystal in all her chandeliers! Wishing a reprieve from her shrill voice, I said little else. It was the pleasantest time we ever spent together.

When the gentlemen retired for brandy and cigars, I sat next to Mr. Bennet and engaged him in a report of his farms. Though laconic, he is intelligent and informed in a bookish way. He is not, however, a master of management, and troubles himself but little with the business of Longbourn farms. It is a mercy the tenants keep so well in fold. He is polite and respectable, and thanked me for my conversation – quite the opposite of his wife. I believe I assisted him on some points of modest rent increases, as his proximity to London permits him to charge more for the use of his land, and heightened land taxes for war coffers will cut in on personal income. It is a delicate balance between generosity and guile, and Bennet, to his credit, leans towards the former. It is not only a lack of sons that has made his family stressed for resources. He told me that his sharpest daughter, Elizabeth, advised him the same!

Determined at least to have Elizabeth look upon me, I found an opening as she poured coffee for the general assembly. I slurped down my first cup and returned with it empty. I braved a smile as my eyes rose up the length of her body. She wore a violet dress in season, and her bodice was low with a line of lace. The hot coffee and summer's breezes through the window gave a fine sheen to her skin. Her hair was carefully arranged in a French twist that accentuated the graceful line of her neck. We spoke cautiously of my sister's travels, then fell to silence, unequal as we were to banal conversation when the line between us is drawn so taut. I simply stood by her for a few minutes to breathe her air. It is enough for now. Between last month at Pemberley and now, the gulf that had divided us is bridged by a friendly hullo. Though I was not satisfied and I daresay she wished for more exchange, we must both live upon crumbs and see whether we salivate for the feast. I still do.

My head is thick with claret and brandy, and the taste of her coffee on my tongue.

1 September   Netherfield Park

Bingley is tizzied with impatience, and is off this morning to call on Jane Bennet. I could hardly keep him on his rump through breakfast. Given the right opportunity, he plans to propose to her. I shall have to wait for his letter to Grosvenor to hear of his success, as I have been wanted in town these three days and plan to leave directly.

Heeler is saddled and stamping in the courtyard. I told Bingley to expect me back within a fortnight and left with my sincerest benedictions on his success. A lover's time passes rapidly, and I will attend him again before he has a minute of idleness.

In the meantime I must decide whether to hazard a second proposal.

2 Sept   Grosvenor Sq.

Smithson, Gibson, and I met in our favoured anonymous watering hole in High Holborn to raise a pint to a good investment. Smithson is positively giddy with the report of Monon, which he has had a chance to peruse in detail. When I say giddy, I mean that his old parched face cracked a smile and he proclaimed that I had not utterly been taken for a fool in the land deal. He brought not the report to the pub, fearing dirty tables and tippy goblets, but we will meet to-morrow at length at my house in Grosvenor.

Smithson then off back to his offices, Gibson and I, more truly friends than steward and master, had a long conversation about

Pemberley's fortunate state amid the general economic and agrarian depression. I had the courage to ask him whether my estate could afford for me to marry a woman of small fortune whom I happened to love, and, his bushy brown eyebrows thrust up to the beams, he promised not to advise me on my finances until I informed him in detail of the feminine charms that would make me a noodle.

I remember my father spending long evenings in his library with old Wickham, discussing affairs much wider-ranging than Pemberley's sphere, and suddenly felt the sweep of generations as I sat back in my booth at unloaded my heart to Gibson. Reciting the whole of my odd, inconsistent relationship with Elizabeth, I see how truly a love story it might be, if only it has the comedic ending. Gibson made me promise to think nothing of tallies, accounts, and cheque-books, when by following my instincts I might find the man inside the gentleman. But a man once rejected! Should he ever propose again? Gibson laughed at the recollection that he proposed to his Martha *thrice* before she accepted him, because she wanted proof that his heart was no fickle organ, but was stout enough to bear the battering of her feminine power of choice.

Have her, Darcy, and make us a new generation of handsome lords and talented ladies.

I was quite content to leave the conversation with that sentiment, and I returned reeling to Grosvenor. I was greeted by a hasty note, half-legible, from Bingley, informing me of his and Jane Bennet's happiness.

3 Sept   Grosvenor Sq.

Smithson came early with a large parcel stamped by the Holland Land Company, and authorized and signed directly by Cazenove, who has returned to Philadelphia. He commissioned and oversaw the surveyor's report, and he sent back half my payment because he desired the land to be better plotted for his own information. It contains ten fair topographical maps of the hundred thousand acre plot south of Pittsburgh on the Monongahela River. It lies west of the highest mountains of the Appalachian range, which splice Pennsylvania along a South-west to North-east axis. The range itself is low, reaching only a few thousand feet, and it is a ripple of long, string-like ridges.

Monon is low upon the river, with ten miles facing the meandering, broad stream, and rights to half the width of the river. One stretch of river front some two hundred by one hundred yards has been cleared of forest, and bears fire rings recently used by travellers – Indians and white men alike. The main part of the land is crowned with stately tall white pine, oak, hemlock, elm, black walnut, hickory, spruce, and chestnut. This primordial forest of titans has never been felled. In the understory are found laurel, dogwood, spicebush, viburnum, holly, and rhododendron. The surveyors make note of some twelve streams leading downhill from the east towards the Monongahela. They are nameless as yet, and presumably unexplored by white men.

The land reaches fifteen miles East-northeast from the river, and this roughly ten by fifteen miles is estimated to contain fifty million mature trees. They would not put a price on the timber, since the river is yet unnavigable and there is no way to remove it, but such timber would fetch an astonishing fortune in England, so desperate are we for mature trees to work into navy ships. Smithson was quite salivating over the timber alone, and said boisterously that I could gift five enormous trees to every soul in England and Wales. But I demurred from these avaricious schemes. Where forests are felled, whole realms fall away, and I shall not allow the will-ye-nill-ye hacking of this American wilderness. Among animals they espied hares, deer, elk, foxes, coyote, red and grey squirrels, black bears, and a panther.

Cazenove suggests that I grant land rights to a few settlers with families, and allow them to live on the land, build cabins, hunt the wild life, and farm a small plantation. If I grant these rights for five years, he will draw up an agreement that limits the land they may clear to ten acres each, and I may chuse whether to renew the contract after the lapse of five years. This plan has the advantages of protecting the land from poachers, keeping a front against Indian encroachment, and further familiarizing me with its features, besides giving these people a livelihood. Their proximity to Pittsburgh would allow them to seek help in extraordinary circumstances. I am inclined to agree with his suggestion, but I'll have Smithson draw up the contract so I may be particular in its terms.

Inhabitation and development must be carefully planned. Though our little lives run roughshod over the landscape, earth abides, and it is our station to leave the land better than we found it. This forest, planted by nature's hand and entirely uncultivated by man, is so different from Pemberley's planted, designed, cultivated forests – not merely the geometrical ranks and rows of the arboretum, but also the pet wilderness on the hills. Monon sets my mind racing. It is a new frontier for the Darcy landscape; I am the hinge between the old English and new American branches of my family.

Will my children chuse a salty pioneer's life, or a London gentleman's?

4 Sept   Grosvenor Sq.

Today I received a letter from my Aunt -- a livid, choleric heap of hatred. It seems that she has been beating all of her informers for intelligence to confirm or refute a rumour in circulation: that

I am secretly engaged to Elizabeth Bennet. She cited the sources of Mr. and Mrs. Collins, my cousin Fitzwilliam, and even Georgie – all of whom were in no position to deny, absolutely, my feelings for the lady. She extracted from Collins his full knowledge of Elizabeth, and was obliged to report to me that the upstart girl had rejected an offer of marriage from him, tho' her acceptance would have kept the family estate in the female line and assured the security of her mother and sisters. Has ever breathed such a selfish, unfeeling, headstrong girl? My Aunt is ashamed she ever deigned to look on her with toleration. She now sees Elizabeth's visits to Rosings as nothing less than pollution, the like of which shall not be aired from the hallowed grounds until I am married to Anne. I am commanded to relate at once the utter falsity of these dirty rumours by an express letter, and she wishes me to attend her at Rosings as soon as I can dismiss my obligations. I am to spend the whole of autumn in the company of her daughter. What can I mean with such obfuscation and delay?

I have in the same mail received letters from Fitzwm and Georgie, both apologizing for revealing anything that I might have wished to keep discreet. Their feet were in the fire. Fitzwm's words turned towards implying that the game's up for me, and I must either defy my Aunt or deny my heart. Can my arrangement of her youngest sister's marriage have had any other aim but than to recover Elizabeth's legitimacy? And what is all this about Elizabeth at Pemberley last month? Has there already been a second proposal accepted? The poor fellow sorts through a scattered bag of puzzle pieces.

Georgie politely suggested that I might relieve my Aunt only through complete honesty, for truthful communications, however painful to their recipient, can tend towards no eventual evil. In matters of the heart, concealment is the surest indication of self-doubt. And she is lonely at Pemberley with no sister to help her wade through the difficult passages of Beethoven, and no companion to instruct her on how to teaze me.

Both of them said that, whatever my intentions, they thought Miss Bennet ravishing. They actually used the same descriptor.

I shall let my Aunt's letter gather dust for a few days. Perhaps her anger will boil down to a gentle simmer, if no new fuel is added. I have no honest response that would not spark fire.

9 Sept   Grosvenor Square

I was nearly run through and scalped by my Aunt today. She walked straight into my house at Grosvenor and wringed Bloom until he informed her that I was at my club. What a surprise to have the predatory dowager, adorned in a leopard fur and crane feathers, stalk into the gentleman's club scattering those gents like rabbits from her path. I was her prey, and she cornered me at last in the library. Fortunately, I had fortified myself in anticipation of this assault, and I was able to divert her spears and actually use them to my advantage.

She accosted Elizabeth last night in her own house. I hardly suppressed a smile as she spat out a relation of the scene that ensued, wherein Eliz refused to promise never to become engaged to me. Though my Aunt admitted that she had but little sway over that blackened girl, she came at once to London to remind me of the full force of her influence over me, as a kind of symbolic mother to her orphaned nephew. I replied that if she was my symbolic mother, it would be indecorous to marry my symbolic sister, Anne, and besides that it would be repulsive.

I followed this too-strong word with a steady narrative on my complete lack of romantic feeling for my cousin, who is a good sort of girl deserving to be happy. I begged that my Aunt ask her daughter of her own wishes for her future, without overpowering her with expectations. I appealed to my struggles, my scruples, my deliberations, and my sense of responsibility to family, and yet how all these obstacles had fallen under the sweep of my ardent feelings. I then related the reasons for my true passion for Elizabeth, which I have felt with the utmost force for the better part of a year. I told her that Elizabeth had never courted my favour, and was completely innocent of accusation that she is an upstart Siren. I have never seen my Aunt destitute of words, but she was quite silenced as the realization of her lost clout settled into her brain. By the end I was left merely to trickle water on fading coals.

We sat in *bergères* by the fire. My Aunt mumbled in a scattered fashion about Anne's illness, the decay of Rosings mansion, and the burden land taxes in Kent, and I heard her attentively, but with no rejoinder. Before long the club doormen guided my Aunt from the prohibited rooms, and she was yet cast in a trance of horror as I called her carriage and sent her packing to the hollow rooms at Cavendish Square. Her fallen face, no longer livid but now simply old, painted an awful portrait through the carriage window as it rattled across the cobblestones, drawing her to an afterlife of broken entitlements. She will be a different woman in future; perhaps a kinder one. If she accepts my choice, I will buoy her.

Elizabeth's defiance gives me hope, as I had scarcely allowed myself to hope before. She is not absolutely, irrevocably decided against me. Her character is too forthright to play at that *charade* simply to frustrate my Aunt. I will hasten to Hertfordshire and place me back within her regard, so she may chuse me *en fin* or release me to some other, lesser life.

11 Sept   Netherfield

There is no happier man in the kingdom. Elizabeth will be mine. We are resolved. I have traced her face with my lips and whispered my troth in her ear. We are in exstasies.

Need I detail my sartorial care on the morning of returning Longbourn? I was arrayed in a thin white linen jacket with a saffron silk shirt and a matching cravat. Bloom set me up with the new fashion of pants that extend to the ancles, and so rather than long boots I wore lighter, square-toed leather shoes. Bingley hung at my doorframe for a half-hour begging me to make haste so we might shove off for Longbourn, as he had promised his *fiancée* to meet her as soon as she set down her breakfast fork. I was biding my time, arranging my thoughts.

We arrived at the house, and directly set off again for a walk through the fine late summer day. Bingley and Jane languished in the pools of each other's eyes, so I forged ahead sandwiched between two Bennet sisters: Elizabeth and Kitty. The three of us hazarded only a few banal remarks on the fine day and the farmer's strident labours in the hayfields. Before long, Kitty escaped us to her friend's house, and Elizabeth and I walked alone together. Bless her, she began our reconciliation. She has long been informed of my part in Lydia's marriage, a secret betrayed by the bride herself, and she thanked me gratefully on behalf of her family for my pains, expense, and self-sacrifice.

This was my opening. I said I had thought only of her; I told her my wishes were unchanged and I needed but one word from her to settle our relations forever. I believe she was shaking even more than me, but she shored herself up and responded that her sentiments had undergone so material a change as to receive my proposal with gratitude and pleasure. I turned to her, stopped, held her two hands and fell to one knee. I delivered a thoroughly shoddy, garbled, and totally honest avowal of my undying love, of the delightful torments of the past eleven months, of the revolution of my soul that she had precipitated. She laughed. The sparkle in her eyes, the lightness in her step, the dimples on display – all of her is my own! As she is mine, I am hers.

I know not where we walked. We wandered on planet Earth, in our own dear kingdom, county Hertfordshire, across hayfields, through meadows, along riffles to cool shaded pools, from the high road to the broken cart-lane, through mud and puddles, among the leaning trees of Longbourn copse, and at last across the bowling lawn behind her house, and in the back door. We resolved a thousand points of awkwardness in a long ribbon of truthful kind words. The ill-breeding of our relatives is counterbalanced; the kindness of our friends is doubled; past resentments shall be shredded and burned. From the ashes of past, old mistakes shall as the phoenix rise to glorious accords. There is a beautiful congruence to our minds, and where we read situations differently, we have each come to understand the other's view. Our first impressions may have been gross manure, but those mistakes of apprehension have nourished the growth of our later regard. Mistakes have been our deliverance.

We kissed goodbye in the copse beside the house, and I left for the evening with Bingley. Each day there has been cause for celebration, but my friend had no notion of what news would crack across his dining table tonight. He was incredulous. In love with her since November? Silently in love, whilst he wheedled away his own broken heart past the endurance of a block? Proposed to her in April, and rejected? Arranged Lydia's marriage? His mirth was so great that the shock of his extreme ignorance, and my active concealment, fell to his mind as comedy, rather than blackguardry.

Bingley and I laughed ourselves to tears, we laughed until the moon smiled back; we laughed until the Netherfield servants suspected madness, and came to look through the key-holes at these two silly lords. I caught one house-maid espying, and called her at once into the saloon with all the force of my gravity. Bingley called the rest of the servants, five in total, with Howe sternly at the helm. With his countenance yet held, Bingley delivered a severe speech on the impropriety of eaves-dropping, and promised to redress the situation by immediately dismissing them all to …a week's vacation with pay, and the promise of steady mirth including two weddings when all commoners would be called to wassail. He order the cellar to be deprived of three bottles of champagne, and the seven of us sat cozy as cats in the open summer night, confessing our loves to each other until the drops were all drained. It was monstrously improper and delightful.

I desire no head-ache in the morning, so I have stayed waking the last hour writing a faithful account of my day – my glorious day. The moon is set, and the sky is jet.

12 Sept   Netherfield

Elizabeth and I walked to Oakham Mount today. We soaked in the rays of sun and the hazy view back towards London. We were afforded the poet's perspective, perched high above the little lives of men below. A few curious sheep kept company with us, as we unpacked our lunch from a basket my bride had prepared and I hauled: bread, cheese, pickled cucumbers, small beer, and lingering kisses. We spent half the day in that spot, playing the pastoral shepherd and his lass. In adventurer's news, I have discovered a birth-mark on her left calf in the shape of Wales.

Her thoughts turned more serious as she contemplated the business of asking her father's permission, for fear that he would be distressed by losing her. My solution was to ask Mr. Bennet for his blessing at once, and to assure him in the same breath that he would have open access to our lives in Derbyshire, or wherever we chose to make our home. I would not deprive him of his daughter, but rather endow him with more options, and God willing a flock of grandchildren in Elizabeth's image. I did so this evening, and it was all soon resolved between father and daughter. Elizabeth plans to tell her mother of our happiness to-night – perhaps she is at it this very minute.

Bennet's countenance wrinkled with confusion and mild displeasure as I began my explanation of my love for his dear Elizabeth, and her acquiescence to my proposal. He assumed she felt duty-bound to accepting me, having rejected Collins, and the protective father vowed not to have his most beloved daughter swept away by a pile of prejudicial pound-notes. He was quite aroused in indignance.

The only way around his displeasure was to bid him ask his daughter her feelings on the matter, and then he might see how her dislike has been swept away. He told me, If she agrees, Darcy, I have no business refusing my consent. I pray that you will make it your mission in life to preserve her happiness. She has no equal in my heart. I bowed, withdrew, and allowed Elizabeth's eloquence to shift the old man's mind to our favour. They both emerged from the library after a quarter of an hour, and tears of delight swelled old Bennet's eyes.

18 Sept   Netherfield

I have been a lazy diarist these last several days. The world's concerns are far removed. Shunned are books, newspapers, pamphlets, and village criers. I have been lingering in a space of pure contentment, thinking and acting very little. Each day brings new insight Elizabeth's keen, teasing, generous mind, and arouses my sympathy for the plight of her family. Even Mrs. Bennet, over-awed by the intelligence of our betrothal, has grown mild, and speaks only in praise and compliments. In the absence of her prattling, Mr. Bennet speaks more of his reasonable opinions, Mary evolves from sententious to sensible, Kitty giggles only at true follies, Jane shines benevolence upon us all, and Bingley conducts the conversation by promising mirth and manna. He brings to the household a new gift from Meryton each time he darkens the doorframe. Mrs. Hill began to have trouble fitting Bingley's baubles on the sitting-room mantle, so he turned to ordering meats and teas for the Longbourn pantry. Today he made a present of a ten-shilling box of fine spermaceti candles, and Mrs. Bennet spent the whole of dinner marveling at their blinding clear light, as if, she said, she were being drawn up to Heaven by divinity itself. My bride remarked that seeing divinity in the head-junk of a great sea beast was a rare devotion indeed, and she hoped her mother would not follow Jonah's example.

In our walk after dinner, Elizabeth informed me that she did once have a brother – nearly. There was a sixth child miscarried, a son that Mrs. Bennet carried for about six months before he was still-born. Elizabeth was only eight years old when this calamity shook Longbourn. In her mind it marks the moment when her mother turned her reproductive energies into match-making ones. She is a woman of prodigious nervous energy, and despairing of any more children, her central object in life was to find rich husbands whose means would counterbalance the loss of Longbourn estate. At that time Jane was but ten years old. Her mother saw an early bloom of beauty and began to circulate the girl in local company. Jane's forbearance, modesty, and salubrious nature are all the more wondrous with this history of forced display.

This was also in this time that Mr. Bennet's estranged uncle completed the legal entailment of the estate over to his son, Collins. It was a nasty time for all, and Mr. Bennet and his brother-in-law Phillips, a solicitor, were repeatedly called to Chancery to defend the estate and beg more time to produce an heir, but to no avail. Once the legal lightning was over, Bennet retrenched to his library to ride out the domestic thunder, which never has abated until these last few weeks. With each passing day Elizabeth and I marvel at the youth returning to her father's figure.

We look forward to some variation with the arrival of the Gardiners in three days' time.

22 Sept   Netherfield

Though he was quite astonished at the mission, I employed Elizabeth's uncle Philips to draw up a marriage agreement that connotes her some of the rights that English marriage law does not provide to females. We have pushed her freedom beyond the legal limit. She has a formal, witnessed document that could be used in court to defend her person, her property, and her rights to divorce in cases of my abuse or infidelity. Philips knows not whether the charter would make any difference, and by letter Smithson proclaims that it is not worth the parchment we used, but still it is the best we can do in this primordial stage of equality. It is a symbol, at least, of how I wish our marriage to be – a partnership of equals. We signed it today, and it will be ratified with our marriage license, and put away in the deposit boxes in London.

The afternoon we wiled away at lawn-bowls, with ladies versus gentleman. Bingley, Gardiner, Bennet, and I took on Kitty, Mrs. Gardiner, Mrs. Bennet, and Elizabeth. Jane served at the side-line, showering us all with compliments, however imperfect our performances. Like her sister, Kitty has energy and a keen eye for the "kitty" well-coordinated with her hand, and the two younger ladies evenly matched the two younger gentlemen. Among the elders, Mrs. Bennet totally overwhelmed the skills of her husband, but Gardiner had stamina and spinning skills that outmatched his wife. Gardiner was the skip for our team, and his final bowl won us the second set. The tie-breaker went to the ladies, two-to-one, and the gentlemen were therefore by our opening wager obliged to assist Mr. Hill in bringing out refreshments.

I stole Elizabeth away behind a stout elm tree in the midst of the rearrangements, and rewarded her victory with a kiss.

23 Sept   Oakham Mount

> Mistress of my soul, here rest your bones
> Secure within the circuit of my arms.
> Ignore the busy world and its alarms
> That buzz us back to marching with the drones.
> The courtier was wrong to hang a sonnet,
> Sad idyll of the lone devoted fellow,
> Upon the ideal grace of cold Stella –
> The she-ghost ne'er undresses, gown and bonnet.
> We may then count ourselves among the blessed,
> To taste this noontime, quiet and unstressed.
> No business stirs us to a zealous rage,
> No heart-ache rattles in our fleshy cage.
> The path I wander starts at your bodice,
> And leads me southwards to that land of promise.

26 Sept   Netherfield

We have been to London and back, seeing about the business of getting married – the license, the presiding clergy, and the honey-moon. We are planning a safe and modest trip to the Lakes, where she has never been. I associate her satirical spirit so closely with that picturesque region, I was quite immovable on the idea once she struck it. Perhaps we may collabourate on some descriptive sketches scenes, where she takes on the middle and remote vistas, and I concentrate on the lady in the foreground.

I have received a letter from my Aunt humbly requesting that she and her daughter be included in the ceremonies as supporting family. She says little else, and I know not her full intentions, but Elizabeth is willing to hazard a scene at the ceremony, because she thinks it much more likely that my Aunt will behave herself when chastened by the serious and awful business of a wedding. She wishes to have that formidable lady back in good graces. We have put her on the list, recipient of one of the fifty gilt invitations Gibson will to send out this week.

The wedding date is settled – Sunday the 8th of October, and we have less than a fortnight to make final preparations. Bingley and Jane have agreed to wait another week, so that we each have our day. Elizabeth and I agree that we desire as little trouble in the preparations as possible, with so many eager hands clamouring to assist us. Gibson is assigned to disbursing funds, so I may be sure they are spent with liberal prudence. Mrs. Bennet and her younger daughters are assigned to the flowers and appointments for the church and the reception at Netherfield. Bingley's cook and my own Mrs. Bursted will let no one else near the feast planning. Bingley's gang of friends from London plan to riddle the deer park for fresh kill. Gardener is selecting the champagne and wine at his favourite shop in Cheapside. Bloom has traveled to London to assist Mrs. Gardiner in the selection of suits and the bridal gown, and has promised to return with several choices in the latest fashion for us both. Mr. Bennet prepares his wedding toast in the confines of his library.

By avoiding all the prattle, Elizabeth and I sequestered several hours entirely for ourselves this afternoon. I swept her away to my private chamber at Netherfield. Though neither of us wishes to make defeat of her bloom before we are officially married, we are both so worked with desire that we nibble around the edges of culmination. I was the drunken bee in the cup of her petals the whole long afternoon. She has tiny curls at the back of her neck; her skin smells of powder and daisies; she has freckles on her shoulders from secret afternoons in the sunny garden; her arms and legs bear fine downy brown hair; the small of her back is a cove just fit for my lips; and her slender ancles curve to the arch of her feet and a family of perfect toes, which I examined individually. We made a thorough inventory of each other, half-undressing in our work, and she was glad for my year-long exertion with the iron pan, as it made my chest a broader pillow for her ear as she counted the lunges of my heart within. We laughed at our marvelous stupidity, and cried at the quivering wonder of this new intimacy. As darkness settled, we lit no candles, but felt our way into night.

I bore her on Heeler back to Longbourn, where we raided the pantry for cheese and cold meats. She dismissed me with a kiss at the front door. I rode him for three hours more in the neighborhood before finding fatigue enough to retire to my chamber.

What revolution is come in eleven months since I first arrived to this same chamber on that frosty wet night, sick of life and packed with *ennui*. The stage is set for our comedy ever after.

1 October   Longbourn

This volume of blank pages is now filled but for one, and he has gifted it to me. Though a wise man has said it is not the fashion to fit the epilogue in a lady's dress, I accept my office and will shift for myself in this wild, windy space. I am a girl turned lady, and I must find my voice. A lady's epilogue depends more upon the lady, than on her story. She might rehearse the errors, contradictions, and perversities of the old year, her brow furrowed in devotion to self-improvement. She might smile in remembrance of the follies that made way for sheer luck in her tale, and laugh herself into another bright day. I am more the second creature.

A good memory is unpardonable when it tracks the bitter breath of spirits past, like a damsel stalks in a draughty castle. Lady Catherine's bitter breath is long aired from our garden path. I recall very little of my first regard for George Wickham, though we are now content to live with him in one kingdom. My memory is even less intact when I think on the past of my future husband, except that he has always been a fine, tall figure with noble features and a satirical eye. What of the long, blank days where I hardly stirred out of doors whilst my gentleman was cavorting in London, or basking in the arms of a French lover? Certainly such sinewy action is beyond the allotment of most women, who must work a fine brush over a small canvas. But any resentment of such differing experience is mere vanity. The events of his chronicle recorded in these preceding pages lie just behind my own quiet story, and give it a texture and relief that shakes the monotony of a woman's life. The dull flats of that quiet canvas are forever riven and quaked by the promises of tomorrow.

My gentleman opens the horizons of my future, and asks me to adopt Derbyshire as my home, London as my society, and America as my horizon. The lady's performance, not of conscribed accomplishments, but of lively, defiant spirit, is here rewarded by lifting me out of that former life and giving me the tools to forge a fresh future in a new century. Wealth never hurts – my mother is eloquent on the subject of privation. Health, vigor, is much prized by its possessor – my father's library became his chamber of convalescence. Beyond these involuntary gifts is a more weighty virtue that anyone might grasp – a durable optimism for fellow man and the patience to let life play out without judgment. There will always be fools, sops, toadys, cheats, gossips, and misanthropes. If one but chuses to sympathize with their pain, and find amusement in their foibles, one is a good way towards happiness.

My life is a link in a long chain. Now that my circle is joined with Fitzwilliam's, the chain of the future may be forged. With delight we turn to our smithy!

The adieu is charity itself.

Finis

www.ingramcontent.com/pod-product-compliance
Lightning Source LLC
Chambersburg PA
CBHW070323130626
46556CB00007B/2709